# LOST TRAIL

## BY NANCY McCARVILLE

**DORRANCE**
PUBLISHING CO
EST. 1920
PITTSBURGH, PENNSYLVANIA 15238

Dorrance Publishing Co
585 Alpha Drive
Suite 103
Pittsburgh, PA 15238
Visit our website at *www.dorrancebookstore.com*

ISBN: 978-1-6495-7149-6
eISBN: 978-1-6495-7658-3

# CHAPTER 1

Activity always seems to happen most for me around 2:00 - 3:30 A.M. My crew and I are investigating an abandoned county home in Iowa. It is over one hundred years old.

When they built these structures, it was always in the middle of nowhere, so if someone got out or decided to run away, there was nothing but miles of corn fields.

Some of the residents were mentally unstable, homeless, or veterans returning from WWI and WWII. Today they would be labeled having PTSD for the men and domestic abuse survivors for the women and children. The year was 1878 when it opened and closed in 2010.

There were many deaths here due to neglect, suicide, illnesses, or abuse. The name of the facility had changed five times because of government funding or donations from rich families that were embarrassed by a family member ending up in the facility.

There have been many paranormal investigations since 2014. When the facility closed, it became for sale. A husband and wife who are from the eastern United States are retired professors of history and loved the property. They bought it and thought of turning it into a venue to rent out for parties, celebrations, and other purposes. The grounds had a very large yard front and back of the building. There

1

was nothing but corn fields surrounding the facility. The building had very large rooms that were wards with many beds. A large cafeteria with an industrial size kitchen. The front door opened to a grand room with beautiful woodwork.

The problem was that the walls and other furnishings represented a stereotypical haunted hospital. There was flaked paint all over the walls, the institutional green color, and the stale smell of years of despair. I could see the vision the owners have, but the amount of work is immense.

When they bought the property in 2014, they moved into a house in a small town that was about eight miles away. There was a small college, and the man has picked up a few classes to teach to supplement their income.

Renovation started in a room that was the entertainment center. There were tables, games, and this is the only room that there was a T.V. They started clearing that room first. It was on one end of the main floor. The walls were getting scraped of their paint, sanded, and they had to use extra precautions due to the paint being lead-based.

One of the first duties was to clear out any usable furniture from all the rooms in the building. The woman, Sue, was walking up to the third floor and where the stairs came to a landing to turn up the rest of the stairs. She looked up and a young girl was standing there at the top of the stairs on the third floor.

The young girl was dressed in clothing that reminded Sue of the thirties' Depression era. Sue stopped in her tracks. Her heartbeat was pounding in her ears. The breath left her body and she had to force herself to breathe. Sue called out to her: "Hello, who are you?" The little girl turned to her left and ran past the wall.

Sue ran up the rest of the stairs to try to talk to her. Sue was new in the area, so she thought maybe a neighboring farmer's daughter wandered on her property. This was concerning since the closest neighbor was over a mile away.

Sue got to the third floor and did not see the little girl. She thought the little girl must be fearful that she is in trouble. Sue called out, "My name is Sue. Please come talk to me; you are not in trouble. Let's be friends." There was dead silence. "Please come out and talk to me. I don't want you to get hurt. This place is very dangerous. There might be loose floorboards."

Sue walked slowly going in and out of the four rooms that the girl could be hiding. She would go in a room, look behind doors, in closets, and under beds but there was no sign. Sue started to get a little angry about the girl being in their building and refusing to come out. She knew if she voiced her irritation, she would never get the little girl to come forward.

Sue knew that the only way out was to go by her at the stairs or the metal fire escaping out one of the windows. She knew that if the little girl stepped on the fire escape, it would make a very loud clanking noise because it was coming loose from the mortar on the side of the building. Her cell phone was in her pocket, so she called her husband, who was in the back cleaning up the grounds. He answered and Sue told him to come up and help search for this little girl. They were afraid she would get hurt, then the idea of the parents starting litigation against them was the first on their mind. The well-being of the child was a priority, but Sue knew she wasn't hurt.

He got there; Sue told him to stay by the stairs as she went from room to room. He was not a mean man, but he was very tall, had a goatee, and a deep voice. He had all the makings of an intimidating presence. Sue went from room to room, checked the window where the fire escape was, nothing was disturbed. They talked, and she started thinking she was just tired and hallucinating. They walked into the room right across the steps and she knew this room had a history. An elderly man lived there until his death. The rumors were that he was gay, but in the forties, that word was not used nor was the lifestyle even allowed to be thought of, especially in the farmland of Iowa. He was angry, a very unpleasant fellow. The talk was that once he died, the atmosphere in the room became very toxic. People would get dizzy and nauseous. They think he died of stomach cancer, and people would say these were similar to the symptoms he would experience.

Sue and her husband walked into the room after failing to find the little girl. Their train of thought changed, hoping the girl got out somehow and was safe. He was talking about the bedroom furniture left there. It was a bed frame with bare springs, a chest of drawers, and a dresser with a large mirror attached to it. The mirror showed some age, getting cloudy on the edges but still in good shape. If they sold it at auction, it would bring a couple hundred dollars for the set.

The couple stood in the room talking about the plan of what to do with the existing furniture. As they were talking, they stopped fretting over the little girl. They stood in the middle of the room, pointing and planning, and Sue started to turn slowly around. As she started to face the mirror, she saw the little girl in the reflection. She appeared to be standing behind Sue and in front of her husband. Sue gasped loudly, turned around quickly to see the little girl. There was no one but her husband. He looked at her as if she saw a mouse, she showed that same reaction. Sue told him that the little girl was standing behind her because Sue saw her in the mirror. "Didn't you see or feel her?" Sue asked him.

"No! There is no one up here except you and me." He was starting to get anxious because if she was going to be this jumpy as they just started the renovation and the goal is two years away, he thought they would never get anything done.

Sue was getting angry; not at him but at the situation. She is not a panicky-type female, except for mice. He caressed her shoulders and turned her toward the mirror thinking he was going to prove a point. As they turned, they both saw the little girl. Sue said in a whisper, "Please tell me you see her."

Her husband said in a soft voice, "Who are you? Where do you live?" He thought to himself—live? That was a stupid question. The young girl did not have a look of happiness or anger, but a look of depression or sadness. "Is there anything we can do for you?" He heard a ghost hunter on T.V. ask that one time. The child looked at them or it felt through them, staring, her skin started to turn pale, patches of rot started appearing on her face. She opened her mouth wide like she was going to scream, but nothing but dirt and smoke or dust flowed out. The mirror started to shake.

Psychologists say that the human mind will react two ways when confronted with fear: fight, or flight. Sue and her husband found another one: frozen.

# Chapter 2

In 2018, when we spent the night at that facility, Sue told us about her first encounter with the mirror. Then she went on to talk about other things occurring, such as knocks, shadows, and objects being thrown. The activity picks up as more cleaning happens. They talked to some people online that are paranormal investigators and advised them to get a digital recorder and see if they can capture an EVP. Experts say that spirits do not like it when the living does renovations to their dwelling.

They followed the advice given about using a recorder and they have received several EVPs, voices, over the next several months. Most of the time it is a little female voice. They have said things like, "Can Suzie come out and play?"... "Get out of my room." ... "Dirt" ... "I want to go home." ... "GRRRRRRR," and many others that it is impossible to make out what they are saying. They posted their EVPs on a website they created about the history of the building and the future plans. But as the EVPs became viral in the paranormal world of investigators, more and more groups would call and ask to be able to spend the night and investigate. Sue and her husband first said no, but then one of the people who suggested the recorder told her, set a price, get a signed release from everyone, and start renting this to investigators. You can make any rules you want. One of the most common rules is "NO OUIJA BOARDS." They came up with a price after investigating other sites such as the Villisca Axe Murder House and put it on the website.

The place started booking more and more days, to the point it was booked months in advance. It was better than a B&B because there was no bedding or linens to clean, no meals to prepare.

This is where we come in. I work with a group of women that all share in the fascination with the ghost hunting investigations. We live in Iowa and Villisca is only two hours away. Villisca is the location of the famous ax murders. In 1912, a family and two, young visitors walked home after an evening church service. It was sometime in the middle of the night that the mom, dad, and six children were hacked to death by an ax. No one ever was found guilty; it is still a cold case.

I actually grew up twenty miles from Villisca. At work one day we were looking at the website of Villisca Murder House. Kelly said, "Why not?" We looked at each other, five other women said they would love to go also, so we booked our virgin night of diving into the paranormal world. I never said I believe 100 percent, nor don't believe, but I do love to be entertained and I started ghost hunting as a way to entertain myself. I love Horror movies and performing in haunted houses for Halloween. I have always had a huge interest in the Catholic Church's power and lore in fighting evil.

When I was growing up, I had a black and white T.V. in my bedroom. Saturday nights at ten-thirty, Omaha had a scary movie host that would play classic movies. The Dracula movies starring Bela Lugosi made me sleep with my hand over my neck. I guess my hand had supernatural powers. I was totally entertained by fantasy, horror, sci-fi, and religious powers. Our first adventure was five years ago. Now we are at the abandoned county home in the middle of corn fields. They have been visited by hundreds of curious people and serious paranormal investigators. The activity seems to be continuous at any time day or night. The activity has been captured via digital recordings, photos, or other electronic devices that measure electricity in the atmosphere. We decided to book a weekend ourselves. It was a weekend in October. It was raining the entire time we were there.

We arrived on a Friday evening, around seven o'clock. The owners gave us a tour all over, describing the types of claims of activities. She mentioned that in the last couple of years, they stopped all renovation due to the huge numbers of reservations to investigate. But in the last six months, some activity has changed. She has never felt threatened until lately. There has been a shadow man showing up more often in the boiler room and rocks or steel bolts have been thrown at people. There have been minor injuries due to this. Sue did not know why this activity has changed. She is fearing the danger could either stop the revenue of people staying or something evil is moving in. If that is the case, then no one could renovate, stay, or rent the place in the future.

# Chapter 3

We settled in, picked a room near the front door as our head-quarters. We unpack our supplies, batteries, equipment, food, and most important, our warm blankets. It is dark outside, so we grab our flashlights, recorders, cameras, spirit box, and rem pods. We start to walk around the ground floor first. There is a wardroom that has eight beds in it. This is a huge room with large windows. This is the room where the young female voice has been recorded saying, "Can Suzie come out and play?" There is also a teddy bear that lights up if it detects changes in EMF, temperature, movement, and vibration.

We got EVPs of a girl mimicking me asking about Suzie. It didn't sound evil but didn't sound shy either. This concerned me but I didn't say anything to the group. We also noticed the teddy bear had lit up two times. We waited around for thirty minutes, and nothing more happened.

We went upstairs to other rooms. There was a room where a WWI vet lived. He was badly injured, was sent to this facility and hung himself in his closet. We spent ninety minutes, and nothing happened.

It was time to return to base camp to review our recordings, snack, warm up and plan our next move. We had been at base camp for forty-five minutes when we heard footsteps on the fire escape out-side. The owner had told us that some teenagers had broken in a few weeks ago and vandalized the place. We all worked at a high school, so I personally wasn't scared but welcomed the challenge of confronting teens. They hate it when they can't scare adults.

We broke up, two of us ran outside to see if there was a vehicle, two went out the back door to the bottom of the fire escape and myself and the last woman, Kelly, ran upstairs to the room where the fire escape connects. My adrenaline was flowing. I was ready for a showdown. We got to the room; the window was not open. Kelly opened it and looked down, she yelled at the girls at the bottom and they didn't see anyone.

I looked at the floor, since it was raining there should be footprints but there was none. I wanted to "debunk" this, so I stood outside on the fire escape, went down a few steps and back up, crawled inside to see if footprints would be left and yes, I did leave footprints.

Kelly and I looked at each other, didn't have to say anything, we went to the floor below us thinking they crawled in the window of the second floor, we were on the third. We ran into the room; no prints and the window was locked from inside. We exhausted a search around all the rooms with no success and went back to base camp. There was lots of chatter and speculation as to what we heard. Was it human? Was it paranormal? I couldn't think of a way to debunk unless it happened again. We placed a camera on the fire escape on the top because that is where it would be protected by the rain.

We got our composure, exhausted as many theories as possible. My theory was that teenagers or drunk "good 'ole boys" parked a mile or so away and walked up here to have some fun. They are sitting outside laughing their ass off. That thought lightened the mood to where we were able to collect our composure and get ready to head out to a new area.

There was talk of a Shadow Man that lurked around the boiler room. This made me think of Freddy Kruger. They called it Jerry. The records showed that there was a maintenance man who worked here around 1920s and he and the head nurse got into a big fight. He never came back to work the next day or ever. There was nothing disturbed in his apartment, everything was still there. They searched, called authorities, but he never did turn up. There were some reports written that the head nurse, Hilda, was nasty. She was very mean to her staff and the patients. It was just after WWI, so they were packed with residents. The owners never turned anyone in need away, so they were exhausted, and this made Hilda impatient of things going wrong or taking longer than necessary. I guess one day Jerry was trying to fix some indoor plumbing, a luxury. A child had dropped a stuffed animal in the toilet. The bunny needed to pee, too. The repairs were taking a very long time, the main water had to be shut off, the animal had gone down quite aways in the pipes. Jerry worked alone, so this was not going to be easy.

Hilda had had it. She started yelling at him for being lazy, incompetent, and said it was no wonder he lived out here alone. She was screaming that he was an ugly monster of a man and he was just a waste of space. He was always a quiet and polite man, the people witnessing this were waiting for him to unload on her. He stood up tall: 6'5" to her 5'5", squared his shoulders, everyone was waiting for shit to hit the fan… "If you think you could do better, here." He shoved the pipe wrench into her gut and walked out. No one saw him leave the building. She stood there with an ugly expression on her face, one of shock and anger. After he had left for about two minutes, she took off running in his direction. Many people wanted to follow but the staff stopped everyone. But they couldn't stop everyone talking about it.

The next day, there was no Jerry, but Hilda was in a very good mood. Some of the staff said she must have gotten laid. This made everyone laugh. The water was still not turned on. They called a plumber from the nearby town instead of waiting for Jerry.

Days, months, and a whole year went on, no one was hired, the apartment was not cleaned out. No one in power seemed to care that he was missing.

This is the type of story that leads to the paranormal world giving legs to rumors. I would love to find true evidence of ghosts, but I also would want it to be 100 percent credible.

We got our equipment together and started to head downstairs. The boiler room was through the kitchen and cafeteria. We stopped in the cafeteria for a while to spend some time there. I kept feeling something like spider webs dragging across my head. This is supposedly a sign of a spirit touching you. But I thought, this is a very old building in the middle of farm country, the bugs and mice are migrating, so I just figured I really did experience Mother Nature instead of a spirit. Kelly shined a flashlight to see if there was a spider web, but we couldn't see anything. I thought that maybe I knocked it down when I waved my hand over my head when I was feeling the sensation.

I wanted to try something. I moved a few steps over, checked for webs over me and bugs first. There was nothing, so I turned on my digital recorder and started asking questions. I wanted to see if a voice would answer me and if I get that same sensation again. "Are you trying to get my attention?" ... "Did you live here?" ... "Why are you still here?" ... "Do you know where you are?" I have discovered it is best to say a question and give the spirit time to respond. They can't communicate as easily as they did when they were alive. If so, there would be no mystery.

After a while, I listened to the recorder in my earbuds right there on the spot. There were intelligent responses, not to every question but to the group of questions. "Yes" seemed to come from a faint female voice. "Died," the same voice said. "Won't let me" was the next answer, same voice. We wondered if that was answering the why are you still here question.

I decided to get my spirit box out, I was excited. I have captured EVPs before but nothing like this. According to the journals left by past investigators, no one else has either. Every place has journals for guests to document their findings.

The spirit box screeched to life. I really hate this noise, but it is a good tool. I asked, "Who is not letting people leave?" We waited. "Why can't the girl go to Heaven?"

A loud, angry sounding male voice blurted through the spirit box, "I need friends!"

I looked at everyone, I was thinking we were going to get something evil, but it sounded sad instead. "Why don't you leave?" The same male voice responded, and it was very difficult, but we think he said, "Nowhere to go."

"Can't you go to Heaven?" There was nothing. We waited, kept asking, "Who are you?"... "Are you Jerry?" ... "Do you like to hang out in the boiler room?" ... "Can we help you?" There was nothing. This might sound discouraging but in the paranormal world, it was amazing. It was definitely an intelligent conversation.

Shelly said that we should go on to the boiler room. We waited for almost an hour after the last response. It was just after 3:00 A.M., and we seem to always have some action around that time. For years I always thought midnight was the bewitching hour, but what I have read, watched, and experienced, it is around three. Three knocks or three scratches are believed to be an evil force mimicking the Father, Son, and Holy Spirit.

We walked into the boiler room. There were five of us. I personally believe more happens when there are less people, but the feeling was one of excitement and if something happened, everyone wanted to be there to witness it. We didn't have much fancy equipment.

The boiler room was large but not much empty space. There were huge pieces of equipment, a furnace, water heaters, and many things that I didn't know what they were. There was the old smell of oil. The dirty grime one would expect in a garage that works with engines.

The others and I would throw out questions every now and again, many of them repeated. We turned a light on because of the danger of maneuvering safely. I positioned myself, so I could see out the door down the dark hallway. It was getting to be around 4:30 A.M., and I was getting tired. I didn't want it to end but it is difficult when you work all day and try to stay up all night. I finally said out loud, "Thank you for talking to us. We are getting ready to leave so, please, give us one more thrill, finish this…" I knocked the "Two Bits and a Haircut" knocks without finishing the last two knocks. We waited about twenty seconds and clang-clang. It came from inside the boiler room. Wow, we wanted to believe it wasn't just some random heater noise. April walked over to the furnace; it was never turned on. We knew it wasn't, but the rational mind starts to come up with ways to scientifically explain the supernatural hints.

I said out loud, "If you want us to stay, or to help you, speak into this device in my hand. If we don't hear anything, we will leave." I let it run for three to four minutes quietly. That is difficult because all the ladies wanted to talk.

I played the recording back, first listening through my ear buds. My whole body jumped. It was the loudest and most direct response I have ever heard myself or ever heard from any of the famous ghost hunters. The recording was played for the others, and the response was loud and desperate: "Bury me, I am here."

A couple of the ladies started to get a little nervous. I got excited. I asked, "Did you die in this building?" We knew there were no records of his death or moving or anything. I am taking that on face value. No one here was sure of his last name. There was an article years ago with a theory that a spirit uses as much energy as it can get just to say one thing. There have been so many responses, maybe he ran out of energy. I had a device that would print out words from questions. It had a five-thousand-word data bank that supposedly spirits can manipulate to respond to questions. "Is your body here in this building?"

A word came on the screen: "Under."

"Are you buried under the building?"

"Basement." Whoa! I couldn't imagine a body being here for ninety years and never being found. But technology is so much more intense. Would police investigators think to try to solve a disappearance through spirits? No, they wouldn't.

I had a temperature gun that measured the air temp. I walked around seeing if there were any cold spots. The whole night was cold but having a digital reader would help us get a starting point. As I walked around, the other ladies examined bricks and flooring to see if there was any part that seemed newer or of different material or lesser quality.

I circled the basement pointing the device around me very slowly, waiting to see if it would change. At the very same time, April noticed something at a spot where I saw the temperature change fifteen degrees colder. We had gloves on, and we rubbed the dirt away from the area in the cement floor and the brick wall. It was in the back corner behind a very large furnace that didn't look like it was used for years. You would have to crawl back there just to see.

April was using her flashlight and noticed the flooring was a rougher texture than the entire rest of the floor. There was obvious water damage in the past and parts of the floor had been replaced.

We called the owner of the building, shared our information with her. If you have ever tried to get the authorities to believe there might be a dead body under concrete and the way you found out was by a ghost, let me know how you did it.

It was 6:00 A.M. by the time we showed all of our evidence to Sue. She didn't really know what to think. For one thing, how to explain the suspicions based on a ghost hunting group of women was not going to be met with respect. I don't think it has anything to do with being women, it is the ghost hunting that is not met with instant respect. When we tell people what we do on the weekends and summers, the response is, "Wow, really? That is so cool," but they have no desire to participate and secretly I think the impression is that we are nuts. I told the other ladies that I would stay with Sue if she wanted to call the authorities. I was very happy I had my own car, so the others did not have to wait. I asked Sue to wait on calling law enforcement and give me time to research some information to support a theory as to why there might be a body in the basement. I went into the town and went to the public library. I researched information about Jerry and a woman named Hilda who had a nursing license and anything else to add validity to the rumors. I found records from the County Home in the archives at the library. I discovered Jerry's last name and Hilda's last name. The date in which Jerry last worked was found out by timecards. No severance pay nor unemployment documentation was found.

The timecards uncovered something interesting, Hilda must have gotten married just a few days after Jerry went missing because her name change was made on the payment vouchers.

I looked in the records of marriages and sure enough, Hilda married a local plumber. The fact that he was a plumber made me suspicious. This plumber was the one they hired to fix the plumbing when Jerry disappeared. There was an invoice for concrete on that same work order. This seems logical, was Jerry jealous? Did he know Hilda was seeing this plumber and couldn't stay there? But all the reports were that Hilda was a nasty piece of work.

If Jerry is buried under the floor in the basement, my mind can see how it would be possible. But the why is another mystery. I couldn't let this go. I got a hotel room in a nearby town and started going to nursing homes to ask about this Plumber. It took only a few different people questioned before I found a group of gentlemen playing cards that all grew up in the area. They remembered the entire thing.

They remember the plumber, Hank. He was not a pleasant person to be around. He was good at his job, but his personality was as nasty as the shit in the pipes. He also was filthy; he didn't get to a shower very often.

They remember when Jerry disappeared. Everyone liked Jerry. He was so generous; he would give the shirt off his back if you needed it. He was not very intelligent. In today's school, he would have been a special ed student. Jerry had a great work ethic and loved people and people loved him.

The men I was interviewing remembered Hilda also. She did not grow up here but came for the nursing job. Everyone in the community was gossiping about how Hilda was fired from so many other institutions that this was her only option left. A small mid-western home out in the middle of nowhere. She did not come into the community much since she had an apartment there on the grounds but when she did it was obvious. Hilda would go into a store and be so rude and impatient that some of the sales ladies would cry because Hilda would humiliate them.

When the news broke of Hank and Hilda marrying and her moving him out to the institution as the handyman, the people were shocked. There was never a time that anyone ever saw them together. This was so unusual that the running joke of the town was that Hank must have had something incriminating on Hilda and he forced her to marry him. Hank was somewhat of a pervert in the community.

This information made me think that maybe Hilda killed Jerry, begged for Hank to help her since he had the reputation of a nasty person, so she thought she could convince him to be quiet. Women have married men and had sex with men for less.

I have always had a strong sense of "woman's intuition," so I was going to try to convince Sue to push hard for the ground to be examined. The concern of a body outweighed the possible embarrassment for Sue. I drove by myself, so everyone else left to go home and I stayed and waited for a deputy to come out and speak to Sue and me. I felt anxious about trying to get some experts to take us seriously and at the same time I knew these were strong findings.

The deputy arrived, he knew Sue luckily for me since we didn't have to explain who she was or that she was the owner of the property.

19

We went to the basement and I proceeded to explain our experiences and I played the evidence we collected from our recordings.

He was very respectful and didn't treat me like a lunatic. I then showed him where the concrete was different from the rest of the floor. He said that he could not justify the department spending money on digging up Sue's basement for the IDEA of a possible body. He said that Sue could do whatever she wanted and if she found evidence of bones to call him back.

Sue and her husband decided to discuss the matter. I downloaded the evidence for them. They had some decisions to make. I told them about geologists using echo machines to see under the ground. The University of Iowa or Iowa State University might have equipment to help with this.

I left before anything was decided. There will be phone calls to them later to find out their decision.

# CHAPTER 4

We posted our recordings and personal experiences on YouTube and Facebook. Since the news broke out about our discoveries at the County Home, we went viral. The owners of the building were able to convince professors to have interns use the echo machine from University of Iowa. The students thought this was just going to be a practice looking for ground water, or artifacts from Native Americans. There have been several arrowheads found in this area in Iowa. The owners asked the professors to not tell the students what the suspicions were, so they would not have a predetermined picture in their minds.

The team arrive during the spring and it took them all day to set up their equipment. After just five hours the next day, the students had evidence of a skeleton.

This started several dominos starting to fall and more ground being checked for more bodies. This made national headlines although the major networks did not really go into the discovery's origin, supernatural recordings. But we did. The Criminal Investigation Agency based in Des Moines, Iowa's answer to FBI, were brought in with excavation tools, cadaver dogs and went to work. They did discover a body. They knew it had been buried for at least fifty years and was a male. Since Jerry was not very well known and lived in the county home, there were no belongings to get DNA. But the skeleton was given a burial and it was marked with Jerry's name. The owners of the building used this story and had a plaque made telling of the research. The reservations grew to where they were booked two years out.

Several different paranormal investigating shows would call us and ask about doing an interview. We did a few but didn't get carried away. My choices were the guys from the Travel Channel. There are two shows that we did. We were invited to participate in a Halloween special at a prison in Missouri with one of the shows on the Travel Channel.

We still viewed our get togethers or hunts as Girls' Night Out, but we were able to request places now that were not rented to the public. That was the best part of this. It was like we were allowed to veer off of the tourist plan. All of this attention was overwhelming at first, then started to feel really proud. We were famous, in the ghost hunting world. Although not famous enough to make a lot of money on this event, it was nice to be able to make connections. We all had to keep our day jobs.

As all of this attention lasted for almost a year, it started to calm down and return to normal. We made some great connections around the nation but our call to stardom had died away,

I had received an email about my upcoming class reunion in my hometown. This is when a person starts to think, how much weight should I lose? What should I wear? I was the same. I was really feeling good about my accomplishments, not just the paranormal notoriety, but the rest of my life. My children, my normal career, and overall health. I decided to plan on attending. It would be nice to catch up, see the old school, talk about things that happened in high school, and just enjoy the visit. No responsibilities, just fun. There was one thing that would be talked about and that one a major event that shook the whole state.

As I drove back to my hometown, I reflected on how my senior year in high school went. How could something so horrible as a missing teenager start with something so fun and in all accounts, very innocent. I am a middle aged school administrator that grew up in a small town in Iowa.

My childhood was very much a Norman Rockwell influenced existence. There were picnics in the town park. We, as children, rode our bicycles everywhere, to the swimming pool, to the lake, each other's houses and we even were doing this at night without fear.

In the summer as pre-teens, my best friends and I would ride our bikes to the park where the swimming pool is. The whole town seemed to be there every day, all ages, the cool high schoolers were lifeguards, the school jocks were there but I don't remember them ever getting wet. I guess when you only had three T.V. channels and PBS, there wasn't a lot of desire to stay inside. Heck, VCRs weren't in the households yet.

We would ride up town, we would go to my dad's office and bum money off of him. I never was told no. The only time I remember being told no was when I rode my motorcycle on the highway without a helmet. Whew, I had never seen my dad that mad, to this day. My mom, yes, but Dad, no. As my friends and I would walk out of his office, I always got the feeling that his secretary had the opinion that I was a spoiled brat. Yes, spoiled, brat, hmmm maybe? Only other people can answer that.

We would stop at the drugstore soda fountain and order Zombies to drink and then look at the newest magazines. I liked comic books. I don't believe anyone else was into them as much as I was.

Some days we would ride over to Carla's dad's Conoco gas station. Carla was our group's very gifted athlete and brain. She liked to fix tires at her dad's place. She was a stud. When she and I were riding around, we would stop there and get a (glass) bottle of Pepsi out of the machine. I really miss glass pop bottles.

In the evening, I would ride over to Darcy and Sherri's house. They were next door neighbors to each other, both in my class and always had fun things to do. There seemed to be a lot of kids our age in that neighborhood.

We would play "Annie, Annie Over." There are two teams, one on each side of the house. You would yell "Annie, Annie Over" and that meant that you were throwing a ball over the house. If the ball failed to get over the house they would have to yell, "pigtails" and attempt again to throw the ball back over. The other team would have to catch the ball before it hit the ground. If they missed, they would have to yell "Annie, Annie Over" and try to throw the ball back over. If they did catch it, they would run around the house and try to capture people from the other team. When the first team would see the second team running around, they had to run to the other side of the house without getting caught. Then the whole process would continue. The object was to eventually capture everyone, and no one would be left on a side. Once the ball made it over the house, you never knew if the ball was caught or not until you saw someone running around to capture you or you heard "Annie, Annie Over."

Connie and Carla were my closest friends out of the group. Carla was the jock, Connie was the beauty, and I was…somewhere in the middle of both. We were really pretty close to all the girls from our school. There were only thirty-three total students in our class, so it was not difficult to do. Before we got our driver's licenses, it was difficult to spend time with the country kids, but once we started driving, we would drive all around town and the country roads on weekends and hangout together.

There was a road between Lenox and Clearfield that was called Roller Coaster Road. It was gravel and if you got the car up to at least sixty miles an hour, you would fly over the three to four steep hills in the mile stretch of Roller Coaster Road. Our stomachs would get that flipping feeling, our butts would fly off of the car seat, it was definitely an adrenaline rush. Nobody wore seat belts back then. I don't remember ever running the road during daylight. That is probably how we survived. At night you could see headlights and know if there was oncoming traffic. As an administrator today, I would lecture against actions like this, since that is the politically correct adult response expected. But it is fun.

`Everyone in our class grew up together. There might have been a couple of kids since Kindergarten that moved away, but it was extremely rare to have a family move in. Our whole town thrived on farming. My dad was an insurance and real estate man, but 90 percent of his customers were farmers. There was no industry except for maybe in Creston twenty miles away. We would make comments about things going on and everyone was knowledgeable about what was being talked about.

There was one girl who moved into our town when we were in junior high, Katie. When we were juniors in high school, Katie was considered the new girl even after being a member of our class for five years. Katie was not fitting in with us. She was one of those kids that would try really hard to carry on a conversation but would end up saying things that were queer or goofy and she would get eye rolls from us. Her dad was a customer of my dad. We ran into them one evening coming out of Dick's Bar and Grill from eating dinner. My dad had a nose that required laser treatments due to diabetes. Katie just blurted out, "What is wrong with your nose?" That pissed me off.

I wanted to yell, "What is wrong with your face?" but I held my tongue.

Katie's hygiene was not very good either. She had very dark hair, really bad dandruff, and she had body odor also. We were showering after PE one day and Sandra, one of our friends/classmates, was very rude towards Katie. She would put extra deodorant in Katie's locker with a note taped to it saying to use it.

Sandra was also very vocal. But she would say things out loud, so everyone, Katie included, would hear her. It would be something like, "OMG, that smells just like someone we know!" This would be after a science experiment when the gas from the Bunsen burner would stink of sulfur. In the girl's locker room, we were required to shower after PE. Katie would hide in the shower, but we never heard water turning on. Sandra would act like she was addressing one of us and yell, "Everyone should be showering; nothing worse than crotch smell in the classroom." I hate to admit I laughed at this behavior. Katie's smell bothered me as well. No one else needed to say anything because Sandra did.

Someone must have complained either about Katie's smell or Sandra's words because she was called in the Principal's office. From that moment on there was a female adult in the locker room. We assumed it was to make sure Katie showered but as an adult, I am pretty sure it was because of the bullying we did to Katie.

I was at Darcy's house and we told her mom what had been going on. Her mom told us to be more understanding, she knew the family and they were very poor and may be limited to the amount of water due to money. We all loved Darcy's mom, Jane. She had the personality of a wise person with a great sense of humor. I heard her speak once at a women's club meeting at the church and she was fun to listen to.

We told the rest of the girls that, but it didn't help. I remember comments died down, but no one really wanted to be near her. I have to wonder if any adult at the school ever talked to her about hygiene. I know we would have today at the school I work.

The rest of the girls that were in my class were seven girls who lived in the country, seven girls who lived in town and then Katie. There was no "wrong side of the tracks" in our small town. Katie lived on the west edge of town. I remember the house and it was small, lots of kids toys outside, and I believe more than two generations resided in the household.

# Chapter 5

Our group had a wide variety of personalities. Donna also was one of those girls who were very secure in her skin. She was smart, didn't worry about what other people said or thought. She never seemed to get worried or upset. She didn't concern herself with being popular or wanting to hang out with us every day. I remember her never eating lunch at school. She would never brown bag or eat school lunch. My stomach was growling in class, so I couldn't imagine skipping a meal.

`Lynda would let me copy off of her schoolwork. She lived just half a mile away from the school, technically in the country. Her dad was an alcoholic and her mom was a Jehovah's Witness. She could never come to our birthday parties or participate in school celebrations. Lynda would have us over sometimes to spend the night. There would be so many of us that we would all be sleeping on the floor in the living room. In the middle of the night, her dad would come home drunk. I don't think any of us ever talked to her about his. We just pretended to not know anything. The worst thing I remember about her dad was one day during lunch, they were having cow's tongue. He wouldn't let me leave without eating some. There are still nightmares.

I am fairly intelligent but only when I was interested in something. I loved basketball, having fun, but didn't really care about studying very much. It is funny that I am a Dean of Students at a high school today. Maybe my experience helps me work with kids that aren't interested in the National Honor Society or school all together. I have never been all that interested in the National Honor Society in high school. If I wanted to, I could have been an A student. I got a straight A's when I got my Master's. But the National Honor Society really does nothing for the high school students. It is just a list of names that get an extra tassel or cord on Graduation day.

Someone would have a slumber party a few times a year and invite everyone except Katie, she would never be invited. She made us uncomfortable to be around her. I really don't know if she ever knew about our gatherings, but I am sure she did. We would rationalize this by saying she had a big family, so I am sure she is playing with her brothers and sisters. This was such a stupid reason, but we did not want her there.

Every time we did have a slumber party, we would play around with seances: "Stiff as a Board, Light as a Feather." One time we lifted a girl with only our two fingers all the way to the ceiling. We would go outside and after dark, do an older version of Hide and Seek. We loved thunderstorms. We lived in tornado alley in Iowa, so storms happened a lot.

When we would hear strange sounds in the middle of the night or go to the cemetery, since Connie lived next to it, I was the front person to investigate. I think because I was the tallest, not the bravest. I can't remember how Connie got out of it. We would try to stay awake all night long. Some of the girls did every time but some slept every time. We would pull practical jokes on the ones that fell asleep. We would take their bras, wet them, and put them in the freezer, put whipped cream on their hand and tickle their nose, and these were the people we were friends with. I don't remember anyone ever having a meltdown or getting pissed at our behavior.

Every one of my close friends growing up had a memorable and picturesque childhood, at least it seemed from the outside, up to our senior year in high school.

# CHAPTER 6

One of the games we played several times a year was Lost Trail. We have no idea where it came from, who thought it up, but we played it and always had fun, at least I did. It was only played at night.

Our town was only 1,100 people, not very big in population or in square miles. My house was on the north edge. Connie's house was on the east edge, between two cemeteries. We would always start at one of our houses. We would divide up into two teams. Each team would have chalk and a flashlight. They would start out walking, and every so often, they would have to mark an arrow showing the direction they were going. It could be on the street, sidewalk, signs, trees, or any surface as long as the other team could tell which way the first team was walking. If the first team is to turn directions, they must show that by the turning arrow. They would walk all over town, then after an hour or so, they would decide on what city block they would hide. They would draw a four-point compass arrow diagram signifying that they are now hiding within a block of the diagram.

Once the second team has sat inside the house for thirty minutes giving the first team a head start, they start out by tracking them. The only tool they needed was a flashlight. They would walk and walk until they came across the four-direction compass arrows. The adrenaline was flowing during the tracking. Picture a small rural town, mid-1970s.

There were not very many streetlights. A railroad track ran through the middle of the town that was great for using and drawing arrows on the rails or on the ties. Another favorite way to go was up and down allies, and we always felt safe, but it was a sure way to make one's imagination run wild with shadows. Now that you are searching all over the street, if you go more than a block, you get worried you might have missed one of the arrows. We would backtrack search sidewalks or the trees, then every time you would find an arrow, it gave a sense of satisfaction.

Once you find the four-direction diagram, your team would decide who would go where to look, do you go together, or do you separate? Once you find a team member, each person would have to run back to the original starting point. So, if the whole team would find just one person, one of each team member would take off as the rest would continue to search before they could start running. When the first team would decide to hide, they have to strategize on if they should hide close to the starting point because they can't run well, or maybe they hide across town because most of the members of the first team are better long distance runners. You never know how it will play out. The first entire team to make it back to the starting home (base) wins. The only thing we ever won was bragging rights.

There were a few favorite hiding places for everyone. Our elementary school had one of those metal fire escape slides. It ran down from the top floor at a steep slope but up at the very top, it turned ninety degrees to a little ledge right before the door leading into the sixth grade classroom. It was perfect for climbing up and sitting and hiding at the very top. There was just enough room for two people. If you were on the searching team and the school was within the one block radius of the sign, you could almost bet that someone would be hiding up there. One of the rules though was that you could not start back until you actually found someone, or you were found. We would always try to yell up the slide to try to trick someone into making a noise. A flashlight would be shone up the slide to see if we could see a foot sticking out. If the hiders were thinking, you would sit up there, legs curled up, hand on mouth and wait to see if the searcher would actually climb up or not. Some girls would always chicken out when it came to climbing the slide, at night, in the dark, because once you turn the corner, you might be face to face with someone, or not; you could never see until the very top.

Hiding in the cemetery was always my favorite spot. I was always somewhat bewildered at the fear some people have with a cemetery at night. This was a great place with lots of very large monuments to hide behind. If we started at Connie's house, it was a very short run to home base. If we started at my house, it was a long run. It was also on a gravel road, so marking your directions was tricky. This made it even more of a rush.

We were planning a game one Friday night after a home football game of our high school. We were going to stay at my house, and since the game wouldn't be over until around ten o'clock or so at night, it would be good and dark. We were seniors in high school at this point so of course we knew it all. We were the leaders of the school. I was planning this all week with my parents. Mom always worries about silly things such as feeding us. Almost all of us had our own car, so there was no worry about taking them home. Mostly everyone would leave first thing Saturday morning anyway. We would all just come to my house after the game, they would bring sleeping bags, a change of clothes or such in the house, then we would get started at Lost Trail. It was at the beginning of October, so there was a chill in the air, a light jacket was enough to keep you comfortable and it wouldn't be too heavy to keep you from running back.

It was our regular crew, no big deal. This was something we did a few times a year, so it wasn't like we talked about the upcoming slumber party. At least I didn't think so. My dad owned a business uptown, real estate, insurance, taxes, and most of the people in the county and neighboring counties were his customers. I don't care what society says, when farmers come to town and have coffee with other men, they gossip more than anyone. I guess Dad knew the girls from my class were coming to our house after the football game for a slumber party and to play Lost Trail. I didn't even know he knew about it because I only spoke to Mom.

Katie, the girl no one was friends with, and her family were customers of my dad. I guess the Thursday before my party, Dad mentioned something to Karen's dad. The old men were all meeting for coffee in the back of Dad's office. Karen's dad said he didn't know anything about a party. My dad said, "Sure, Nancy said all of the girls in her class were invited. Tell Katie to come over." I didn't know anything about this. Dad didn't come home until dinner at six o'clock. A ritual that was never different unless I was basketball practice. Then he would sit in his chair or go back to the office. I always had a comic book at the table. Not a lot of conversation went on. I was the last child remaining at home and was very spoiled. I *was* spoiled, of course I am a very well-adjusted adult now. At least that is what I try to convince my sister and brother. The point is that Dad did not warn me or tell me about the conversation with Katie's dad. I know he probably didn't think it was a big deal, he probably thought I already knew she was coming since I said all the girls in my class, and she was in my class.

I had never told my parents about the torment we gave Katie. My mother thrives on an image we present to the community. Heaven forbid I would do anything that would impact on my dad's business. To this day, my parents have never spoken about their politics, they never wanted anyone to be upset with them, so it was never spoken of. If Mom knew about the treatment I was involved in towards smelly Katie, I would probably be sent away.

Friday during school, Katie came up to me at my locker and asked if she could get a ride with me after the game to my house, she said she didn't have a car but that her mom would be picking her up at my house Saturday morning. I stood there, mouth open, other girls standing there listening, I really was a fairly intelligent student but at that moment I looked and sounded like "Sloth" from the Goonies. I always wondered if she could tell I was surprised or did my abilities to cover up my surprise fool her. She never did say. I said, "For what?"

She explained that her dad told her that my dad invited her to my slumber party after the game. Katie said she had heard me mention at lunch about everyone coming to my house, but she didn't realize she was included. At that moment she seemed really happy. I have often wondered if she was just clever enough to know how to "stick it" to me or was she really happy. I didn't want to know, so I smiled, I think, and said, "Sure just sit with us during the game and we'll all go to the parking lot together. You can put your stuff in my car before the game." She smiled and walked away to go to class. I just stood there staring as she walked away. In my mind I was thinking, "Shit, shit, shit, shit."

There were about four or five of my friends standing there, they freaked out at me, "What the hell?" There were a small group of my friends that were the "sweet" ones. They told the rest of us that what harm would there be, only one night, we would be outside playing Lost Trail until after midnight, the morning would come quickly. I agreed but feeling very uncomfortable about being around her. Her ability to participate in our conversations was very agonizing. I decided since the party starts at my house, I would pick teams. Whew, I would make sure she was on the other team and not with Sandra.

The day went on as a normal day. I really didn't think anything of it. I was arrogant enough to figure everyone would buck up and have a good time anyway.

# CHAPTER 7

The football game started, it was around eight o'clock or so Friday night. Our team was out there trying to win. They weren't the best, but they weren't the worst in our conference. It was our Senior year, so we all tried to experience every moment of it. Our class only had thirty-three total, and I would say we seemed to bond very well the last couple of years. Now, as of today, we would be bonding with Katie, or at least pretend to.

It didn't bother me anymore that she was coming. I had a plan of how to stay away from her most of the night. Basketball season would be starting in a few weeks and then track season, so I would be too busy to have these parties for the rest of the year. After graduation, I didn't give a shit who was doing what. I had my plan, my summer at the lake, then college. I was not sweating it anymore.

Sandra found me at the bleachers and sat next to me. We all were sitting fairly close to each other. Our bleachers were not very big, so even if you did not want to sit with someone, they were going to be fairly close by. Sandra was our biggest bitcher about Katie. She was the most upset. I always thought this was funny because she was the only one in our school who belonged to a Baptist church in another community. Her religion was very strange to us because in my town, you were either Methodist or Catholic. The word Baptist brought strange images in my mind. She was the most religious in our group. At least, that is what she said.

She told me at the game that there was no way she was going to go to the same party as Katie. I told her who gives a shit if she is there or not. You can ignore her if you want. She was getting pissy about it. I told her if she didn't want to stay, fine, but I was not going to tell Katie not to come. Katie was sitting down on the bottom row, a few of us would roll our eyes about where she was sitting because everyone knows you can't see anything on the bottom row, the players' butts were all you could see. This was the atmosphere prior to meeting at our house. I didn't care, but as I reflect, this had to be obvious to her. She was quiet during the game. She was in our group, sort of, but the conversation really wasn't including her. Most of what we talked about was gossip about each other and the boys in our high school.

Game was over, we lost by six, no shock. We all started walking over to the parking lot by the high school where our cars were. The school was the main focal point for the entire community. The police were directing traffic out of the parking lot. Our town only had two, full-time officers, our own little Mayberry. Whenever there were events involving a large number of people from out of town, the reserve officers would help out with parking, crowds, etc. I believe the only time they were needed were after football games, graduation, the fireworks at the lake on the Fourth of July, and our annual Rodeo which was a three-day event and very popular in the Midwest circuit.

Katie ran up to walk with me. I am sure no one would have ridden in my car with her but since everyone had their own car, it didn't look weird that we were the only two girls in my car. As we walked through the parking lot, the police officers would be giving me crap. I gave it right back, since they were either related to me or good friends of my parents. We would always be joking around. I always thought I would be able to get out of a ticket in that community or county if I needed to, but I never had the privilege to challenge that theory.

I drove home and as I was driving Katie was talking about how she has never been to my house, mentioned something about picturing it being really nice, something about being in the nice part of town. I could feel myself roll my eyes; I swear it was an involuntary movement at this time. I got to my house and the other girls were parking along the street. We went into the house and Mom was still up. Dad had not gotten home yet; he was the official team movie man. It was video by now, but he also did the 8 mm in the past when my brother was playing. It was after 10:00 P.M., and we started pouring out Pepsi, from glass bottles, for everyone and were sitting around the kitchen and family room, where the T.V. was. We were talking about dividing up teams, getting chalk and flashlights ready. I said let's have the first team: Katie, Donna, Sherri, Darcy, Patty, Lynda, and Kylee. Second team: Nancy, Carla, Connie, Kathleen, Pam, Jean, Sandra, and Jina.

This was the best solution for me because Connie and Carla were my closest friends, and this kept Sandra away from Katie. But Kathleen asked me how I came up with this grouping. I lied, said went eeny, meeny, miny, moe. We finished eating the cardboard pizza and drinking Pepsi.

It is strange how you think everyone in your class gets along so well until they have to be with someone that is considered different than your own normal. The only people happy were the ones on my team. I expected Sandra to get nasty when the names were drawn but she kept her mouth shut. Luckily, Darcy and Donna were with Katie. These girls were very nice. All I know is that I didn't have to be on Katie's team. I was happy. Man, I always get my way.

# Chapter 8

We started at 10:30 P.M. after we ate frozen pizza. It was in the low-fifties, low wind, so we all needed jackets but not heavy coats. The first team, the team with Katie, started walking. We stayed in my family room watching a VCR tape of *Smokey and the Bandit*. I was the first one in my group to get a VCR player. We were unable to see what direction the first team started.

The first team was walking down the street making their marks, talking about people, yes gossiping. That is what teenage girls do. They were talking about how Danny broke up with me without telling me. How it was so embarrassing because I had gone up to Danny to ask about when he was going to pick me up for the Homecoming dance. Joleen was standing there, I didn't think anything about it because Joleen talks to all the boys. He looked at me, mouth open, Joleen walked away, Danny said that he had asked Joleen. I said that it was okay, I was just curious because we hadn't talked for a week or so. I tried to hide the fact that I was dying of embarrassment, I pretended I was the coolest chick in the world. I didn't realize I didn't fool anyone. So, that was part of the gossip. Katie would not have any idea about any of this gossip since no one really ever gave her the time of day at school.

Most girls would always do the deep sigh and roll her eyes whenever Katie would ask questions about some of the gossipy stories.

Things were said like, "DON'T WORRY ABOUT IT!" Luckily, at least in my guilt, Darcy would always politely walk by Katie and joke about, "I have no idea either, I think it is…" Patty and Jean were never mean or short, but they didn't really open up either, they would join in and laugh, etc.

Darcy and Sherri were the closest friends of team one. Kylee and Donna were close, but the rest of the girls were friends. Most of the families knew each other, but Sandra's parents were not known very well to any of us.

Sandra's family belonged to the strictest religion, no dancing, no makeup, Wednesday nights were strict church nights, but Sandra did fit in very well at school. She was very pretty, funny, didn't dress weird, didn't talk about religion, but boy Katie bothered her. I don't know if she thought the dandruff was contagious or if the smell hurt her nose? The smell was not every day. As I am so much older and wiser now, I wondered if the smell was during her period.

The team walked for almost an hour. They had gone south for eight blocks, then west for ten blocks, at the very edge of the town. They went back south for two blocks then back east. It is always dangerous to circle because if you go for many blocks then left and left again, you run the danger of running into the second team before you get a chance to hide. The longer they walked, the more Katie would get bold about sharing her thoughts and ideas about where to go. Kylee lost her cool, she strongly expressed that Katie has never played with us before and that she needs to keep quiet about where to go. There was a long silence as they walked. The original plan was to go to the other far end of the town and hide in the cemetery, but Darcy and Sherri suggested using the block around the elementary school to hide. This is a normal place. I had sometimes thought to ignore the arrows and just go straight to the school, but the time I do that, I would have to go back to the beginning and retrace my steps, so I would never do that.

Everyone agreed. Katie asked as they were walking, where are the best places to hide? Patty and Lynda were wanting to know also. They would always be invited to our parties, sometimes they wouldn't be able to come. Some of the slumber parties they would attend were the ones that we did not play Lost Trail. Donna and Kylee would start talking about the best places. Of course, the fire escape slide at the elementary school was mentioned very first. Donna fiercely expressed that she was going to use the slide. No one wanted to argue. There was an outbuilding in the playground that was used as the kindergarten classroom. There were nooks around there. The rules we made up were that you could hide within the entire block of the four, directional arrows. There were some houses on that block that had sheds you could go into. If we did that today, we would be arrested. The school took up most of the block, so it was fairly easy to search the area also.

The team made it to the block where the school was. They drew the four, directional arrows in the middle of the street. Kylee drew the arrows, but she added a flare to it. It did not look like the normal drawing. Everyone split up and went to their hiding spots. One of the more important things to a hiding spot was to be comfortable. It might be thirty minutes or more before the second team is in the area. Donna crawled up the slide, she perched herself on the small landing just out of sight from the ground. She was the first to leave the group to hide. Sherri and Darcy went over to the kindergarten building and slid down in the window egress for the basement window. Patty and Kylee went over to the house that is owned by the local chiropractor. He was gone, so they went to his shed, and Kylee sat in there behind his rider mower. Lynda went up on his front porch and laid down behind the railing. It was not hidden very well but in the dark, we have found out that sometimes the best hiding places are out in the open as long as you are very still. The streetlight on the corner of his house is burnt out, so the open porch is the last place the second team would think to look.

No one asked Katie to hide with them. Many of the girls liked to hide with someone, I always liked to hide alone. People like to whisper, giggle, or constantly talk when the searchers are getting close. I don't like that. The point is, hiding by yourself is not unusual, but to someone who has never played with us before, I assume, was a little frustrating as to where to go or with who. She did not ask anyone; everyone just split and ran to a hiding spot. Kylee stressed before, or as Donna was leaving to go to the slide, you cannot start running back to home base until someone on the other team sees you and yells out your name. That verifies that you were seen, and their eyes were not playing tricks on them.

To this day, I don't believe anyone meant to leave Katie out, they just took off. Remember these are sixteen- to seventeen-year-old girls. By this time, Katie was feeling sad, the walk was full of frustration because of the attitude from everyone. Even though no one else was as evident of not liking Katie, it was obvious that they weren't planning on being best buds any time soon.

Katie stood there in the elementary playground, at eleven-thirty at night watching everyone take off to their chosen hiding spot. She looked around, really wanted to find a great spot for a couple of reasons. She wanted to show everyone that she is awesome at this game, and if it took a while to find her, maybe we would get worried or concerned for her. That would show us. She tried to remember the boundaries of how far she was allowed to hide from the four-way direction arrows. One block from the arrows kept ringing in her ears. The question was, one block in any direction? Katie was certain that was how it was meant. She had lived here in Lenox for several years, so she knew the neighborhood fairly well.

Across the street from the elementary school, there was a house that had been empty for several years. I had always asked my dad why no one lived there, and he said it was because the owner was in the nursing home and there was no family left. It was old, needed tons of work just to be livable. It was next door to my grandparents, so this is why I knew something about this house. My dad had always pretended to be mad at my mom for always giving my sister, brother, and myself a ride to the school. He always said, he walked to school every day, snow, rain, no matter what. Well, Dad lived across the street. He thought this was funny, after the two hundredth time, it was a yawn.

When I was in elementary school, my cousins from Des Moines would come stay at Grandpa and Grandma's for a few days in the summer. I would always go play with them. We would put on old clothes, old shoes (with heels) and walk up and down the sidewalk. Sometimes we would go to the abandoned house next door and sit on the porch swing. We would always try to peek in the windows, try the front door, always locked and trying to see who gets scared first. We imagined we would hear sounds coming from inside. Then we would sit on the swing and make up stories about the house. We would swing back and forth, talking, laughing, then one of us would stop suddenly. "Did you hear that?" This statement would get our imaginations rolling. I swear our minds made up crazy noises and shadows and my two cousins would take off running and screaming. I would sit there on the swing, never hearing what they claimed, but I would look in the window and think I would see a rocker move or hear footsteps. I followed by running away from the house also.

Anyway, Katie knew about this house, she thought why not hide there. This would be brilliant because she was sure no one would think she was brave enough. The house was empty, so she knew no one would call the cop, only one cop in town and he slept in his car most of the time. She ran over to the house. It was getting near midnight and she knew our team would be getting there very soon. She got up on the porch, tried the door just for shits and giggles, and whoa! It opened. Katie jumped. What the hell? She called out, "Hello." There was no answer, she tried again, louder, and firmer, still nothing. The light switch was flipped on and off, nothing. The dust on the floor was shining from the streetlight, it was rarely working on this block. Karen could tell that no one had been in here for many, many months. It occurred to her that my team would be able to follow her steps in the dust.

Katie stepped out of the house and ran around to the back porch. The backyard was very dark, no light from the street because an alley was in the back yard that was butt up to the neighbor's backyard. The neighbor's houses were dark since it was very late. She tried the back door, unlocked. This went into the kitchen. It was obvious that it was a fully stocked kitchen, dishes, pots, pans, and canned goods were on an open shelf. Clearly no human being had been in there for many years. The 1940's refrigerator had mold growing on the door. The stench was warning you not to open the door. The sink and faucet were covered in dirt, slime, and gunk. Stereotypes are created for a reason and buildings are no exception. There are always cobwebs all over a haunted house and the amount of webs in the back kitchen alone was so thick it looked fake. There was thick dust on the floor, but the countertop was right next to the back door. Katie was trying so hard to be clever and she thought she would gain respect as the best hider, the bravest and top team player. Hiding was a big part of the game, but the adventurous part of the game was hearing the other team come near, getting found and racing back to the home base. Since being part of a group was foreign to Katie, she didn't really have a way to know this.

Katie reached for the edges of the countertop as she kept her feet outside the door. She was able to pull her body up on top of the counter. She thought that if she crawled on top of the counter away from the windows and doors, she could jump down and walk into the middle of the house without leaving any footprints in the dust. She thought that we would look into the windows and see no footsteps and give up looking.

She crawled on the counter, moved over the sink and towards the corner of the kitchen. The counter turned 90 degrees toward the doorway to the dining room. There was old green carpet on the floor of the dining room, so she was able to jump from the counter to the carpet without ever putting her foot down on the dark, yellow-brown stained linoleum floor. When she jumped, she landed on her knees on the carpet. Her knees complained and she didn't scream but she did moan very loudly from the sudden impact. It hurt like a bitch. She rolled over on her back rubbing her legs for a couple of moments. Katie rolled up her pant legs to inspect her knees fully expecting to see them disfigured or bloody after that amount of pain, but nothing. It was surprising to feel that much pain and not see any physical evidence, so she thought. After a short while she stood up, wincing. She knew she could walk, but it would take a while to shake it off. Katie limped to the front living room where the front door was. She would be able to see the front of the elementary school from the picture window. She sat on a dusty armchair to watch outside. As she waited, she would look around and see where she would go once someone tried to find her.

There was a wooden staircase that went upstairs. Katie looked at her watch, glanced out the window, decided she had time to run upstairs to scout hiding places. She climbed each step and the wood creaked so loud as to cuss her out for waking it up. In her mind she thought this would be a good alarm if she decided to hide up here. She noticed the upstairs opened up to a large bedroom. The upstairs was too small for a hallway. She looked around the bedroom, looked under the old bed, no room between the wooden floor and the metal springs to crawl. She stood up and walked over to a small door, it was half as tall as a regular door. She opened it, saw that it was an attic. There were not very many things in the attic, some old boxes, an old fashioned trunk, and Christmas decorations from many years ago. As she stepped inside the door, it was very obvious that she could not walk in, the stored items were sitting on planks and between the planks were no floorboards, just discolored insulation.

Katie stepped back, looked around, and saw a closet door. In her mind she pictured hiding in the closet and when one of us would open up the door and look in, she would scare the shit out of us. This thought gave her great pleasure. She never ever acted upset or hurt by our bullying behavior towards her but at that moment, the idea of getting back at one of us was very pleasant to Katie.

She opened the closet door, slowly stepped inside. There was an expectation of clothes or boxes that she could hide behind, but nothing. Not a hanger, a shoebox, or anything. The closet was completely empty. She had started to get a little nervous, but soon was just disappointed. But she thought to herself that hiding in the upstairs closet would be common, an expected trick.

There were other doors downstairs, so the strategy now was to hide where she could watch out the window. Katie went to the main floor, started opening every door, there were a couple of closets and a bathroom, but hiding in the tub was done to death also. She started to get a little bored, noticed that no one was walking around outside yet, so she started to snoop around everything in the living room.

She felt a very large board under the stairs give away as she pushed on it. The board was the size of a small crawl space, it opened up. The position of this was perfect because she could crouch in the space, watch outside and close up the space before anyone would get in the house. She backed into the space and held the door/board in front of her, so she could close it fast.

It was not clear as to how long she sat there before she noticed our team across the street walking towards the elementary school. She could hear us laughing, being crude and she noticed our flashlights looking for chalk signs. We got about half of a block past the old house and on the block in front of the elementary when we saw the four arrows symbol. Katie saw us stop and look around. She could hear us talking and pointing but couldn't make out exactly what we were saying. In her imagination we were saying where to start looking.

Since she was in the only abandoned house in the neighborhood, she just knew this would have to be one of our first places. Each person has to find someone before they can start back to home base. No one hiding can sneak back to home base until someone finds them. No one ever being found was ever a problem, so a way to end the game due to not finding everyone was never considered.

# CHAPTER 9

We ran around to the playground side of the school. I took the fire escape slide, everyone else got too chicken to come face to face with someone at the top. I loved going up there. Carla and Connie went to the shed in the backyard of a house next to the school. When Carla got the door open to the shed, she walked in first. Connie held the flashlight and first looked up since there were exposed beams in the shed. One time someone had crawled up there and jumped down on one of the seekers. I think it was actually Connie herself. In the shed, it smelled of old engine oil, potting soil, and charcoal briquettes. There was a riding and push lawn mower in there, snow shovels, empty pots, hand tools for gardening, lots of junk hanging on the wall and a large blue tarp covering something in the corner. Carla and Connie grinned at each other thinking, "Duh…that is obvious." Connie stood by the door to block anyone from getting out first and held the flashlight while Carla went over to the corner and pulled the tarp up off the mysterious lump. It was twenty bags of potting soil. Not a single person. They thought for sure it would be one of the hiding team members. They walked out of the shed, replaced the hook that kept the door shut and started to walk away. Connie's flashlight panned the back porch of the house and four, glowing circles caught Carla and Connie's eyes from under the porch and behind the lattice. They walked slowly and closer to what looked like eyes glowing in the dark, but they couldn't see if it was human or animal. There are a lot of raccoons that run the town at night.

As they got closer, they could see that Lynda and Kylee were the ones behind the eyes. You would think, why crawl in a spot where you had trouble crawling out, but all they had to do is roll, and there was an opening on the other side of the porch and they could be out at the same time Carla and Connie got around the house. Those four started running back to the home base.

Pam and Jean went around the Kindergarten building, looking under the steps where there is a good crawl space. They did not see anyone or anything disturbed like someone had tried to crawl there. That was the only place they knew of that would be a decent hiding spot around that building. The back of the large elementary school was next to the outer building and there was a large assembly of trash cans. Pam and Jean walked over and inspected to see if anyone was hiding behind them. They shined their light into the windows of the building just to see inside for curiosity sake. We had all gone to school there until ninth grade. They tried the back door of the school, just to see if it could be pulled open. This was long before security cameras or motion alarms. They stood looking around and discussed where to look next. Jean said that since they peeked in the windows of the 1-8 building, maybe they should look through the windows of the kindergarten building. You never know, there was a time last year when if you pulled on the new gym doors at the high school, the bolt would not hold, and you could get in. I had an ex-boyfriend that turned loose some geese in the school one time. That is how I knew about this.

Pam was not a lot taller than Jean, but she still had to stand on her toes to be able to see in the windows. She scanned around the large room, saw desks, posters, floor mats, a piano, and as the light started to scan towards the wooden entrance door, she thought she saw a couple of heads duck down. Pam was an amazingly friendly person, good athlete, but very, very shy. Whenever she was nervous or trying to say something, she would laugh a lot or giggle. Jean was what you would call a quiet cowgirl. She was not involved in a lot of activities but working with horses was her thing. She heard Pam say that she thought she saw two people duck down outside the front door as she moved the flashlight around. Jean listened, thought, then remembered that the front door had something like an old fashioned farmhouse, it had a breezeway. It used to connect to another building, but this building was moved to this location. I remember hearing my parents talk about it back when Dad went to high school in the forties here. There was the outside door, then it was like a very small, enclosed porch, and then a door to the classroom. Both doors were kept locked when school was out. Jean told Pam that maybe the outside door was open, and someone was hiding inside the breezeway. They walked around the building, trying to be very quiet as there was pea gravel under their feet. Pam was quite a bit heavier than Jean, so Jean crawled up the three, wooden steps to try the door, once and if the door opened, Pam would step up to join Jean. Jean would talk like she was a chicken, but she was pretty brave when it came down to it. Jean grabbed the brass doorknob, turned it slowly, but nothing, it would not budge. She started to twist it back and forth, but it would not turn, like it was welded shut. She was about ready to give up and start to look somewhere else, but she pulled as she was twisting the knob and the door gave slightly. Her eyes got big with adrenaline and she looked back at Pam. Pam, as usual, gave her nervous giggle, and walked up the steps to join Jean. They slowly opened the door and stepped inside the porch area. There were never any boxes in that area, just some coat hooks and cubbies to store snow boots. The room was extremely dark because the only window was the window in the door leading to the classroom. Some small amount of light came through that way, but it was very little. The girls turned their flashlight to the right, nothing but coat hooks, and then to the left. Sometimes the easiest way to scare ourselves or others is not to do anything at all. As Jean and Pam looked to the left, Patty and Darcy were just sitting there out in the open on top of the boot cubbies. They were being quiet, smiling wanting to laugh as Pam and Jean tried to find them. Jean screamed and jumped, Pam giggled and they all dropped their flashlights. They started laughing, and then started back to home base. They did not like to run, so they just walked all together, talked about where they were going to hide, where to look, and other conversations about what their respective teams were having. They could care less which team won.

At the same time this was going on, Jina and Kathleen were searching in a different area. They also played this a lot with us over the years, so they knew the traditional hiding spots when the elementary school was used. They figured everyone else would want to try a new place also. They walked across the street to the house that was also across from the house Katie was hiding inside. The house Jina and Kathleen went to was where one of our boy classmates lived. His mom was pretty cool, she was young, loved to help us think of practical jokes to play on teachers, and she was a barrel racer in the Rodeo circuit. All of our moms were stay-at-home, cookie-baking, shocked-at-new-things moms. Typical WWII mom's, at least most of them. Jina knew that if they were caught in their yard this late at night, it wouldn't matter. There was quite a bit of stuff in their yard, not exactly tidy. There were four kids and Ron, our classmate, was the oldest, so there were bikes, boards, golf clubs, dog toys, etc. all over the yard. There was a very large doghouse. Kathleen remembered Ron talking about how they had lost their German Shepherd a few weeks ago. Jina and Kathleen thought that if they were hiding, they would crawl inside of there. So, they stood there, shining their light on the doghouse, frozen, waiting for the other to make the first move. These two were both cheerleaders, straight A students, cute, friendly, funny, and petite. They were the best of friends. Some of the others thought the drawing was rigged since they were on the same team.

There was a large curtain covering the opening of the doghouse, this was to prevent snow from blowing in, so the girls had to bend over to open up the curtain to see if anyone was hiding inside. They push each other saying, "You go." ... "No, you go!" Finally, they went at the same time, pushed aside the curtain, and...nothing. All that build up to find the doghouse empty. They turned around and saw that Patty and Lynda were standing right behind them. They had forgotten that Jean was close to Ron's mom because they were both horse people. In our small town, that was a pretty tight club. Ron's mom was standing there with them, everyone started laughing and Bev, Ron's mom, offered a ride to the home base instead of running, or walking as in the last group. Of course, everyone accepted.

The main fun or excitement of this game was the pursuit of the hunt. The rules were a little weak, but it was fun. I was still crawling up the slide during all of this excitement. I didn't know where anyone else was, I had a feeling it would be easy to figure out. Usually when someone is found, the discovery was yelled out. I didn't hear anything, I heard some laughing and thought to myself in frustration that when I play, I like to imagine I am CIA, or a badass looking for some beasts, or anything to transport me from a small town Iowa. If you are laughing out loud then everyone will know where you are. Man, take it more seriously! I tend to get bossy which led me to feel it was more fun to search alone after we would discover the four, directional arrows.

I crawled up the fire escape slide, with each movement higher, the metal would creak and groan as my hands and knees would climb. There was no sneaking up the slide, but if you would a good hider, you could squeeze in the dark on the top and keep very quiet, so the climber would not know of your presence until they got to the very top. It was very rare to find a good hider to keep from breathing hard or giggling. Every little sound echoed in that metal slide.

I got close to the top, I would stop trying to hear sounds of evidence of someone hiding, nothing. I was confident because I *knew* someone would be hiding up here. I couldn't believe how someone else beside myself could remain so quiet while they could obviously hear someone crawl up the slide to find them. I always held pride in my own bravery. One more move and I would be looking face to face around the corner to my prey. I reached up, the metal groaned and creaked, I leaned to the left, and it is very hard to describe the feeling of intense anticipation to totally let down. There was no one there. How could that be? I know it is the easiest and most obvious place to hide, but it is the most fun for both the hunter and hunted. No one, crap, and of course I insisted on searching by myself. Now what!

I tried to remember all of the noise I heard as I was climbing, I knew I heard Connie and Kathleen's voice. I think I could tell where they found someone. The question now was, is anyone left? I decided to look around the block some more as time went on. I looked in places that were already searched successfully. I know I heard Patty and Ron's mom's voice across the street. The rules were that you could only hide within the block of the symbol. But I suppose those girls who have not played every time might think since it was in the middle of the street in front of the school that this might include the blocks around it. I need to remember to discuss this situation before we play next time.

I walked across the street, looked around the same place that Jina, Kathleen, Patty, and Jean were when they found each other. So much of this was obvious, but it was good clean fun. I walked across the street to Grandma's house, which was next to the abandoned house. I realized I never used Grandma's house to hide in, she and I had a great relationship, but I don't think she would appreciate the thrill of this game. I walked over to the abandoned house, stood on the sidewalk in front and stared at it. I was thinking how much this would be a great place, but others would be too chicken. I walked up to the porch, didn't see any footprints in the dust, peeked in the picture window, but not too long. I always brag about being brave, but to be honest, I didn't have the nerve to stare long. There was nothing jumping out at me or moving shadows, so I said to myself, "Nope, no one would go in there." I didn't go in the back yard because it was slanted, and I was getting tired of being by myself. I just assumed that everyone had been found and all were back at base, my house. I turned and started to walk/jog back to my house.

# Chapter 10

Katie could see us running around. She heard Bev, Ron's mom, laughing with some of the girls. She could see four of them walking away on the other side of the street. It was clear to Katie that they would not be coming to the house she was in. She relaxed; she got a fun sort of anxious feeling when she thought someone was getting close. There was a feeling of pride in herself for being brave enough to come in this house. She was sure this was the type of thing that the group would congratulate Katie on and make sure she was included in things for the rest of the senior year.

Her watch was telling her it was past midnight, she could see shadows and hear some low chatter, but it was obvious no one was coming near the house. Her stomach started growling, she thought, *Oh, great*, as she was hiding, her stomach would give her away. Yawns are starting to come at a very fast pace. She started to wonder if this was worth it. Should she just start walking back to the base? She couldn't do that; everyone would call her a quitter.

Were there any searchers left? Katie imagined herself walking back to the base and EVERYONE being there, eating, laughing at the fact that Karen stayed hid so long with no one looking for her. This was just in her imagination, but we never gave her any reason to think differently. She also thought that she would show them, she would stay hidden, prove to them she is a team player, and not go back until very early in the morning. She thought that my parents would be pissed at the group. Revenge, it might be sweet.

All of a sudden, Katie saw me outside across the street. I was looking around Ron's house, and by myself. Katie couldn't remember if I was by myself by choice or someone was with me, but Katie couldn't see them. She was afraid of being seen from the window then I would have a head start on her running back to the base. Katie was sure I couldn't see her. She saw me stop, look over at the house, and all of a sudden start to walk across the street towards Katie. CRAP! Katie thought maybe she could be seen. She saw me stand in front of this house just staring at it. No moving. Katie ducked under the picture window; she had crawled out of her hiding hole to get a better look. She squatted there listening, afraid to start crawling back to her hiding cubby. She looked above her, she could see that I was standing there on the porch and by the shadows looking in the window. Katie froze, didn't move a muscle, not sure if she was even breathing. All of a sudden, she noticed that I moved away, and Katie could hear by the crunching of the leaves outside that I was walking over by the side of the house. There was no evidence of a second person with me by the shadows or sound, so Katie quickly scrambled back over to her hiding hole under the stairs. She pulled the panel back in front of her but left it a crack open. She was proud of herself for having such a unique hiding place and also that they WERE looking for her. She was so happy at this moment, her heartbeat was racing, goose bumps were on her arm. Breathing was slightly louder than normal. This was the first time she felt like part of the group. The night has not been bad at all, in her opinion.

It was getting stuffy and very warm and sweat was starting to bead on Karen's forehead. It was after midnight, she was getting tired, stinky, and hungry. She closed her eyes, thinking this would give her rest and she could still listen for me or anyone coming in the house. As if there was a supernatural spell, Katie fell asleep, no one ever entered the house.

# CHAPTER 11

It was around 3:00 A.M. Katie jerked her eyes wide open, thinking it had only been a few minutes. She glanced at her watch and saw how late it was and the feeling of sadness, anger, and fear was overwhelming. She said to herself, to hell with everyone, she was going to go home and never speak to any of us again. Her parents were going to be sad though, they were so proud of her being asked to spend the night. What to do! She could just wait until the sun came up and walk to my house and pretend to her parents, she had a good time. She thought of walking to my house and screaming at us for being assholes. This was not her style.

Katie crawled out; it was much cooler outside of the cubby. She stood at the picture window just staring out, remembering everyone she saw running outside, me looking in this house. She was trying to figure out why no one had tried to find her. What were they doing at the base? Were they talking about her, laughing, telling gross stories? Of course, why else wouldn't anyone have found her by now?

Her emotions were strong, more of despair than anger. Her mother keeps her involved with cousins who live in another town, but Katie knows it is just to keep her occupied, so she won't feel left out and alone from her classmates.

She remembers a twin bed, dusty but upstairs and it would give her something to lay on besides the dirty floor. She went upstairs, the only thoughts were to sleep, so the night would end quickly, and she would figure out what to do when the sun came up. As she walked toward the staircase, she felt some rumbling under her feet. Nerves popped up inside her as she thought this was, hoping this was, us just being really stupid. Katie thought to herself that we must have realized we didn't find her, so came back to the area to look. Katie backed into a corner and squatted down to wait for the next sound. The wind was picking up outside and the overgrown shrubbery was scraping the outside of the house like an old crone's fingernails. The old house was whistling from the wind. It was starting to play mind games on Katie. She was feeling foolish at the fact that the natural events of nature were freaking her out. She decided to get up, walk outside and walk home. If nothing else, she would sleep in her sister's room and pretend to come home later in the day. Her sister didn't want her to come to our party anyway. She was sure her secret would be safe with her. She didn't want her dad to get upset with my dad, he had always been very kind to her.

So that was the plan, walk home. She thought that maybe they did look for her, but she was just a skilled hider. Katie got up and started to walk toward the back door. As she stepped across the threshold of the living room to the kitchen, the floorboards buckled. This made her stop, she thought that since it had been so many years since a human had walked in the house that her weight might have caused the damage. She tried to step across the rotten boards with a giant step but as she lifted her right leg, the boards started to break and shoot vertically up like they were stopping her on purpose.

Katie was freaked! She turned around and tried to open the front door, she knew it was locked but she did not want to try to get into the kitchen after what she saw. She grabbed the doorknob, twisted, pulled, banged on the wood, and looked for a dead bolt or something to get the door open. There was no give in the door. She turned around to look at the floor that seemed to vomit wood all of a sudden. She kept repeating out loud, "There is a logical reason for this." Katie was not convincing herself of this. She had always been a demure girl, so breaking a window did not come to her right away. There was a small degree of denial in what was happening. It was really quiet now and our area of Iowa was known for tornado watches and things, so maybe the wind was worse outside than she thought, and it was a natural phenomenon. There was a counter butted up next to the right side of the doorway, so she put her hands on the counter as she leaned through the doorway. There were drawers with porcelain, dusty, pulls on them. She pushed her weight up on her hands and her right foot stood on the pull to try to jump up and sit on the counter, this way she could make her way over the hole in the floor and run out the back door that was open. She got up on the counter, foot standing on the handle of the bottom drawer and she was very weak in the arms so she would have to push off of her foot in order to swing her butt up on the counter. As she bent her knee to give herself a little jump, the porcelain pull shattered and her leg fell down into the tattered boards that looked like spikes outside a medieval castle to spear through the bodies of their enemies.

Her blue jeans pant leg got caught on one of the splintered boards and pierced her calf. She screamed bloody howls. The blood was flowing so fast due to her heart racing. She tried to pull her leg up, but the wood had gone all the way through and sticking out the other side. She started to panic and could not pull her leg out. Since the wood was so old, she thought she could maybe break the board and leave it in her leg. But she was in so much pain, confusion, and freaked out that she was not able to do so. She fell on the floor, no more screams, she tried to compose herself. The drawers behind her back might contain some utensils that she would use as tools. There was no time to waste, a frantic search started. The first things she found were plastic forks, old receipts, dusty towels, and when she was about to pass out from sheer fear, she found a butcher knife. It was a very large and rusty thing, and this made Katie have a small amount of hope. She started to use the knife like a lever to force the board in her leg loose from the floor. That didn't work. The next step was to try to cut the wood like the knife was a saw blade. No progress. She then started to carve away the wood. She was able to make progress splinter by splinter, but it was better than nothing. The blood was still flowing, would she bleed to death before she got her leg out? She grabbed one of the dirty dish towels and tied it around her calf hoping this would slow the blood down.

She was not sure on how long it had been, but she started to get lightheaded and nauseous. She has carved in about ½ inch and still had a couple more to go but thought it was getting narrow enough that she could break the wood. Katie grabbed the massive splinter and with a very loud groan, tried to break the wood at the narrowest spot where Katie had carved it. It was cracking, she started to laugh maniacally and continued to strain to break it. There was more cracking, and it was getting louder and louder. She stopped and realized the cracking sound was not from her breaking the wood but from the hole in the floor. Dirt, mud, and an oily substance started to bubble out of the hole. Katie thought maybe her losing blood was causing her to hallucinate but she reached over and rubbed her hand in the oily ooze and rubbed it on her leg thinking it was going to help remove the splinter. She was maneuvering the oil in the cut in her leg thinking like if it gets slippery enough, it will slide out. Her head was bent over her leg trying to pull the splinter out though the oily mess and she did not see the hand reach up out of the floor. It had a very dark gray toned skin, missing some fingernails, and a filthy arm. It looked like it had been rotting for months. The other hand reached up out of the hole and the arms started to pull their own body up out of the hole. The creature appeared up out of the floor and looked like a demon-possessed female from a nightmare. The hair was either dark or full of mud and oil, long and laying in clumps like dreadlocks. The only part of the face that was visible were the eyes. They were yellow and the teeth were pointed and rotten. There did not appear to be any clothes, but the "skin" was so pale dirty gray, torn, flapping skin, that it was hard to distinguish from torn material to torn skin.

As the creature pulled up, it looked over to Karen. It tilted its head at her like a dog does when you say, "Want to go for a ride?" It looked confused, excited, and started to sniff towards her. This is what alerted Katie about the creature, she looked at it and her eyes got wide, her mouth was wide open, but no sound came out. The creature crawled toward Katie and started to sniff at her leg where the blood was. A tongue rolled out and started to taste the blood. Katie lost her mind, she started to cut at her leg to get herself free. The creature screamed a horrible guttural pained scream and grabbed the knife and tore it out of Katie's hand. It grabbed Katie's head with one hand, palmed it like an athlete would palm a basketball, and started to drag Katie down the hole. The board in the leg stopped the motion and the creature reached up and yanked the leg loose and crawled down deep beneath the house where it came from. All that was left was some blood and skin fragments in the kitchen on the floor. Sounds of muffled chomping, slurping, and agony softly rose from the hole.

# CHAPTER 12

We sat around for about an hour after everyone got back, it was around 2:30-3:30 A.M. We were laughing and recounting the night's activity and the teasing of the ones who were the most scared. We were sitting outside on the patio; it wasn't very cold, but we were waiting for Katie to come back. Didn't anyone find her? No one confirmed even looking for her. We accounted for everyone's location and that I was the only one who came back without finding anyone on the other team. We decided to walk back to the block where we were hiding to look for her. We were actually commenting, "What an idiot to wait this long; obviously the game was over long ago!"

Someone else said, "This pisses me off because now we don't have enough time to switch." We always did the game twice, so each team has a chance to be the ones hiding. Since Katie had not shown up, we needed to go look for her since we were afraid of our parents getting mad.

We walked back to the block where the elementary building was and located the symbol. I looked at it and asked, "Who was the one that drew this? It is not the normal drawing; it was somewhat different." The others said that they let Kylee. She wanted to use some flare. Kylee was gifted artistically and a bit of a showoff, she must have just drawn whatever she wanted. I guess the controlling part of me wanted everyone to use the same symbol. It was close enough that we knew what it was to be telling us when we started looking for the hiders.

We stood around in the middle of the street and talked over everywhere that was searched. I then said I stood on the porch of the old house next to my grandparents and peeked in the window but then left. It was creepy. I got some serious looks from everyone. "What the hell? I bet that is where she is!" said Carla.

I replied, "Who would be stupid enough to hide in an old house that is probably falling down?"

Everyone answered in unison, "KATIE!" We walked over to the house. Luckily, we remembered to bring a couple of flashlights. Going to this house with a group didn't seem as spooky as when I was alone. I thought I was braver than that, I can't believe how much of a chicken I had acted. Of course, she would find a way to hide here, she is new to our activity and she probably wanted to prove how brave she was. DUH!

I walked up on the front porch and tried the doorknob. Locked. We went behind the porch swing and peered into the picture window. Sherri was yelling, "Tie, the game is over! Where are you? We need to get home!" No sound came from the house, Carla, Connie, and I walked around the back of the house, and there was a breezeway, so it seemed like a perfect hiding spot. The guilt of not looking the first time was weighing on me. We walked through the screen door and there was a lot of junk in the breezeway, but we didn't find Katie. The others had joined us in the back. Darcy noticed fresh footprints in the dust going under the back door to the house. Oh, my God! She *did* go into the house. We noticed no prints were coming out. Pam turned the doorknob and it was open. I was going from guilty to pissed that she was in there and would not reply and we had to waste time coming back to get her.

I pushed my way to the front and in a pissy voice, "Katie, this is over! Where are you? If you want to ruin our night by hiding in this hell hole, fine, but we are here to take you back to my house! Answer me!" No sound except some creaks on the floor from all of us crowding around behind me.

Carla showed her flashlight over to the doorway leading to the front room and saw the large hole in the floor with tons of blood shimmering in the moonlight. She called out, "Jesus!" We all ran over to the hole. In a split second we were all envisioning, in our head, her body lying in the basement. We got to the hole, peered down, there was no basement. This was odd due to the time period of these houses either having a basement or root cellar due to tornados or "The Bomb."

Sandra yelled, "Is that skin?"

Lynda, who was very logical and scientific, squatted down and looked closer and agreed it was skin. There was so much blood and the skin was still soft and wet. The girls screamed and ran out of the house. There were four of us who went around the house looking for her, maybe she crawled somewhere and was unconscious. We were able to step over the hole, went upstairs, looked in cupboards, closets, under furniture, and did not find any traces of blood, prints or anything.

We couldn't understand why someone would try to step over a huge, obviously dangerous hole in the floor. I am a lot taller than Katie and there would be no way I would be able to jump over it. The jagged boards looked like brown rotten teeth waiting for its next meal. The only way a person could get past the hole is to climb up on the countertop and leap to the floor in the living room. That was risky also.

We joined everyone else outside and since Darcy lived just on the other side of the block, we went to her house to wake up her parents. They were the levelheaded type. The police were called, everyone's parents came, and Katie's. I had trouble looking at them. The police had to call the County Sheriff's office to investigate. There was a search, the sun was coming up by now. In rural Iowa in the 1970s, law enforcement was sparse.

We were all questioned separately, there was no suspicion from the police of malice or any of us hiding anything. I did hide the fact that I could have looked into the house hours earlier. I don't know if the other girls told anyone this fact, but I did not tell any adult this part. Would I have been able to save her if I went into the house? Or would I be dead also.

The police called in one of the local doctors to look at the scene since the "investigative detectives" for our state were two hours away and they wanted the doctor to collect samples of skin, blood, the dirt under the hole, and any prints were taken by the police. The doctor told the police that with that much blood pooled around the area, no one could survive that unless found within twenty minutes of the injury. The strange thing was that there were no blood drippings anywhere in the house other than that one spot. None of us could see any and I overheard the police stating that fact. We did see footprints all over but no sign of her bleeding.

Katie's family was crying but not screaming at me or anything. They never talked to me. I couldn't look at them. My dad talked to them, helped pay for a memorial service after about a month went by and no luck finding her or any part of her.

The school year went on, we graduated in May, a moment of silence for Katie. The summer came and went, no more Lost Trail was played. We left our town and went to college, never speaking of that night again. There were a few of us that stayed in the town and became teachers or farmers, but it was like if we spoke of it, bad things would happen.

I left, never lived there again. I have always felt guilt for her being gone. They confirmed that the skin and blood was Katie's. I would imagine werewolves taking her away and that was how I explained the missing clues of her body and blood trail. I was imagining ways to live with my guilt, surviving.

# CHAPTER 13

It has been forty years since graduation. My school has an all school dinner for all alumni, but they honor certain years. This year they are honoring twenty-five, forty, and sixty years since graduation. I had not been back to my hometown for many years and really didn't think I would go back even now. Since the invention of social media, many people have reconnected with me from that area. Everyone seems so happy and successful, gotta be a bunch of crap. I grew up hating high school, and, ironically, my career for the last twenty-five years has been in education. My childhood dream was to be a police officer, but my lack of work ethic after high school gave me a different direction. I jumped from job to job. I had some skills at typing, professional office mannerisms, worked in a grocery store, construction office, even at a cattle feed yard. I was floundering and I needed to get back to finding something to be steady, insurance, retirement, and a little respect. I didn't think I was able to do the police academy at this time of my life, with kids, so I went to college and got my degree in education. I eventually became the disciplinarian for a high school.

Strangely enough, my personality was a little "forceful" or militaristic when it came to behavior. Students couldn't ask for anyone who would fight for them more than me, but then again, I won't hesitate to call them out on behaviors and call out parents for their behavior. This got me as close to being a police officer as possible. It is the best of everything I enjoy. I work with teenagers, community, law enforcement, and I get my summers off.

There have been times where I would really lose my temper at a student for being so reckless with their lives. A therapist told me I am still hanging on to guilt for not looking for Katie so many decades earlier. It makes sense but I deal with it as best I can. Having experienced this, I have had a very strange interest/obsession with thrillers and horror stories. I first thought it would just be a way to prove my bravery. Then the ghost hunting shows started showing up all over the T.V. There are some ladies I have developed some friendships with that like those shows also and we started developing our own paranormal investigation group. We would only be able to go to a few hunts a year, but we have our own equipment, we have met some regular hunters all over our state and in a couple of other states. The paranormal society is very small.

Our very first ghost hunt was in Villisca, Iowa at the Axe Murder House. We didn't have much except for some cameras, digital recorders, and a device that would spell out words as if the spirit was speaking. It was in November, the Tuesday night before Thanksgiving. We didn't have school the next day, so we were all able to stay awake all night. It was literally -5 degrees that night. It happened to be the coldest night of the entire winter and winter hadn't even started yet. There is no electricity, plumbing, or water at the Villisca house. They restored it as it was in 1912, the year of the murders. We were freezing. There are always lots of snacks with us at these events. What else do you do at 2:00 A.M. when you are reviewing recordings?

We set up our sleeping bags on the living room floor. We went upstairs to begin, and I had my recorder on. The attic door was at the top of the stairs and it is assumed that the murderer was inside the attic door waiting since there were several cigarette butts in a pile right inside and the family did not smoke. We were talking and one of us said, "Who is going in the attic first?" This was in reference to who is going to be first to step inside the attic.

My recorder captured a very clear whisper: "I will."

As the night went on, we all had some amazing experiences. On the main floor, it was well after midnight and we were all sitting on the wooden, warped floor in a very large circle. We were eating snacks, talking, laughing, listening to our recordings. One of the ladies with me I had known for over ten years and her name is Shelly. I captured an EVP recording of a little girl whispering, "Michelle." I had everyone listen to it and of course they all gasp in delight, shock, and a little nervous. I said, I wonder what that means since none of the six children murdered here were named Michelle.

One of the ladies smacked me in the shoulder and said, "That is Shelly's real name— Michelle!" Oh, my God! I had forgotten. This made more sense because of what happened next.

While we were in the circle, there were lots of rubber balls of all sizes that other visitors have left over the years due to having so many children being killed in this tiny house. The stories are that the spirits of the children would play with the living visitors. Shelly held her hand over one yellow ball and was trying to communicate to the spirits. She was asking if they wanted to play. Her hand was at least five to six inches above and as she moved her hand, the ball would follow. My skeptic part of my mind wouldn't believe this but at the same time, I was in awe. Anna was sitting on the other side of the circle across from Shelly. Anna said out loud, "Can I play ball with you?"

Shelly replied, "I will roll the ball to Anna."

As the ball rolled to Anna, she told the spirits to roll the ball back to Shelly. It did roll. I got a video of this interaction on my iPad. Anna and Shelly would put their hand out to stop the ball but then took their hand off. The ball was rolling with and against the grain and the warped wood without any living person pushing it. This was seven to eight feet across the circle. We all tried to debunk this by saying it was rolling down a hill, a one-hundred-year-old house was bound to be a little crooked. Shelly said, "Roll the ball back to Anna." After several minutes and the ball looking like it was rocking back and forth then it did actually roll over to Anna.

Kelly was sitting on the side of the circle and as the ball rolled back across, Kelly said, "I want to play, too." On this request the ball left from Shelly and turned 90 degrees to the left and went to Kelly. All of us were gasping and actually clapping and praising the invisible force. I examined this, trying to debunk, but it was going up the slant and turned against the warped boards. I was trying to act cook on the outside. This was our first time out ghost hunting and the experiences were amazing. We were hooked.

Whenever we needed to go to the bathroom, we had to leave the house and go to the little museum set up in the little building in the backyard. It had heat, water, and electricity. Before we left, I ran upstairs and placed my digital recorder on the floor next to the attic door. I then joined everyone in the building in the back. I didn't admit to anyone that going upstairs alone was a creepy feeling. I just told myself that I was letting my mind play tricks on myself. We spent a good forty minutes in the museum reading the old newspaper articles, looking at the artifacts of items under glass for safe keeping. There also was a journal that people like us were to record any happenings during our stay. We enjoyed reading what other people had gone through. Many things have already happened to us that were similar to others. We had gone from the cellar to the attic and there was no way there was any electronic rigging or anything to try to trick people. In the twenty-first century, it would be rather easy to rig a place to pretend it is haunted. Crystal and I would build a haunted house every year for student projects, so I am familiar with some modern devices for that very purpose. There was nothing.

We went back to the house; it was probably around 2:00 A.M. by this time. We went to the main floor bedroom where the two visiting children were murdered and started doing some EVPs. The information we read about this room was that one of the girls had her nightgown pulled up and underwear pulled down. There was a large slab of bacon left in the room. It was understood that the murderer used the fatty bacon to masturbate with. Other "experts" disagreed but really didn't offer a more reasonable explanation. All the mirrors were covered by the murderer also. There were several minutes of recording but the only thing we heard was a growl.

There have been mediums visiting the house over the years and have reported that one of the little girls likes to growl at the living to have a little fun. It was 3:00 A.M. at this time, so we went upstairs to just sit and take our time. There were six people murdered in the very small upstairs: mom, dad, and four children. I sat in a closet and closed the door for quite a while by myself. The only thing I caught on my recorder was my own stomach growling. We sat up there for a couple hours. Some of us went back downstairs to try to get a couple hours sleep. The others stayed upstairs.

It was seven o'clock, and we started packing up all of our belongings in our vehicles, cleaning up and getting ready to head home. It was a two hour drive; Thanksgiving was the next day, so we all had things to do. Everyone was outside and I decided to do one more walk around to make sure we cleaned up. As I was walking in the kitchen, I saw Kelly doing the same thing checking over the place one more time. She was in the living room just off of the kitchen. I could see her very easily. There was one of those very heavy pot belly, woodburning stoves there in the living room. Kelly was saying, "Thanks for allowing us to stay here; we had a great time." At that very moment, the heavy cast iron door to the stove swung open towards her. I stopped, frozen, just staring at what I just saw. Kelly was freaking out.

I said, "I saw that! Thanks for giving us signs; we are leaving now." Kelly and I went outside and were very excited and were telling everyone.

This was my first night as a ghost hunter. It was so amazing, I was hooked. I started researching lore and theories. There was equipment to purchase and other groups to share and explore with. One thing about the paranormal societies, they are very welcoming to other people's stories, ideas, and experiments. I was riding the fence about believing and wanting to debunk or find logical reasons. I really think that is the most healthy way to approach things like this. It would be so easy to be taken in by charlatans or drive one mad by accepting anything that goes bump in the night which is usually just wood settling or pipes heating and cooling.

# Chapter 14

There was another group that invited us to investigate with them in a hundred year old hotel in a very rural area. This hotel was next to the railroad that was once the main source of transportation. The tracks are abandoned today. There are photos of prostitutes standing on the balcony in the late 1800s waiting for businessmen traveling from Omaha to Chicago. This is amazing historical documentation. Our wholesome state of Iowa houses a rather successful brothel in a tiny little town of less than one thousand people.

Today, the new owners of the hotel decorated in the time period of the nineteenth century with the exception of there being electricity and heat.

When I arrived at the hotel, it was in December, a couple weeks before Christmas and the hotel was beautifully decorated. The hotel is still used for special occasions, tours, and small gatherings. The rooms are not very big as it is a typical Victorian type architecture. There are twelve guest rooms on the second floor. According to the historical society, there have been over ninety deaths there since the construction in the 1800s. Whenever you get prostitutes, rich businessmen traveling the railroad, and alcohol involved, there would be violence. There were gunfights, stabbings, abortions gone wrong, and suicides. I believe around the 1940s, the travel on the railway died down to mainly freight and stopping in that town for the grain elevator which was only a block from the hotel. This is when the hotel started taking in low income guests and long term residents suffering from (battle fatigue) today it is PTSD. Veterans from WWI and WWII have called this hotel home.

My fellow hunters and I arrived at the hotel around 7:00 P.M. on a Friday night. It was not a long drive, so this was very convenient. The other group that invited us had been there a couple hours before. We saw their equipment. They have been doing this for several years. I thought I was walking into mission control. The amount of batteries, cables, cameras, other gizmos I had only seen on the cable shows was mind blowing. The one lady put a rem pod in the formal living room. This lights up if the electromagnetic field in a 360-degree area is manipulated. A man or woman cannot affect this. I had my own spirit box, a device that sweeps radio frequencies too fast to detect broadcasts but that you can hear spirits in their own voice. I pulled this small transistor looking device out of my bag and they said they have one set up downstairs. It was just like mine, but it was hooked up to the biggest speaker. Both groups had handheld EMF detectors. There were full spectrum cameras, digital recorders, digital cameras, SLS cameras, and one thing that made me think, now we have really gone off the deep end, spirit sticks.

We went upstairs, it was very dark, standing in one of the bedrooms that had a large mirror on a dresser next to a twin sized bed. The full spectrum camera kept getting something from the mirror. This room was said to have housed the owner at one point and he was not a very nice guy. He hated women and rumors had it that he was gay but back in the early 1900s, one would never come out and admit that.

In the hallway, there has been activity on one end where there is a sixteen-year-old boy who hangs out in the corner near a window. He likes to play with people's hair. I went and stood there; cold air started surrounding me. I played it off when we were in Iowa in December. But one of the people from the other group looked through his SLS camera and there was a stick figure standing next to me. I said out loud, "Hello, we are not here to hurt anyone; we just want to visit. Can you hold my hand?" I waited, only a few seconds and I mentioned that my hand was tingly and cold. The whole group, eight of them, were watching the screen and they said he was touching my hand. No one played with my hair though.

We went to the basement and that was where the spirit box hooked up to a large speaker was set up. They said they have communicated with Max many times who died there of natural causes. He tends to be naughty and didn't like visitors, but now he tolerates this other group since they are here a lot. He still likes to mess with new people like us. They started a conversation with Max, mainly one word or two answers only. Women's voices would sometimes come through. One man asked the spirits how many were here, a woman said thirty-five. A little boy came through, the woman with us from the other group said she has spoken to him before. She asked if this was Peter, a yes came through.

Kelly had her digital camera, and she was snapping pictures this whole time and the amount of orbs was mind blowing. It was too cold for any bugs to be around. The EMF detector was lighting up like the Fourth of July over in the corner of the basement. The man who runs the SLS camera came over to the corner and we saw very short stick figures, three sometimes four of them. The woman with us said she has played Ring Around the Rosey before. We asked if they wanted to play today, we started skipping in a circle singing the nursery rhyme and when we got to all fall down, the stick figures looked like they sat down also.

We started to walk back upstairs to the main floor and the rem pod was lit up like a Christmas tree. The older lady with the other group told us a sad story of a WWII Vet staying at the hotel when he came back from the war. He was injured but no one could find out to what extent were the injuries. He was a very well respected man, son of a local farmer but was not able to work on the farm. The farm eventually got sold out and there was no family to pass on the farm too since the veteran was not married and childless. One night, he went into the bathroom on the second floor of the hotel, sat in the shared bathroom inside the claw footed tub and shot himself. This event was confirmed by community records. The woman who told us this story said that she has communicated with him with her spirit sticks before and that the tub up there now was the original.

We went upstairs, all sat in the bathroom on the floor and the woman who had the spirit sticks sat in the tub. She would hold them and say cross for yes, spread apart for no. These looked like the old divining rods one would use to look for water.

She would ask several questions, some personal information about some of us. If there were any spirits here connected to any of us. If the answer was a dramatic yes, the sticks would spin. Many of these responses got the majority of the answers correct based on the personal information. Not all of us had connections, no one in the spirit world knew me. This made me think, I was the only one in the group that did not grow up in the area. None of these people knew anything about my history. My desire to debunk started suspiciously thinking she knows the answers to all these bits of information because they all grew up together. There were two of my friends who the spirit sticks were supposedly speaking to were very emotional. They both had recently lost someone close to them, so I decided to keep my thoughts about debunking to myself and discuss this at a later time.

It got to be around 5:30 A.M. and things had quieted down pretty drastically. As we were packing up our belongings, we all were in the dining room. We continued our talk of listening to the more experienced investigators. The lady that was the leader talked about the rules we need to be aware of if we want to continue this type of "hobby." The biggest one was never to use a Ouija Board. I sort of chuckled thinking that growing up, my friends and I played with one over the years. It was considered a game. She said that the Ouija Board is not a game. It is very serious and too many people can invoke evil entities without even knowing it. A misconception of using the Ouija Board is that if one is to use it, they are to close the door when they are finished. Also, provoking spirits is never advised. When you sign up to spend the night at buildings throughout the country, they make you sign a waiver. Every one so far has stated: 1. Ouija Boards are forbidden 2. Provoking is forbidden. If anyone in our group is caught doing either of these activities, we will be removed from the property and never be allowed back. My skepticism kept me thinking, a mind play to get people excited to make money by selling nights to paranormal groups. But I later got on the internet and searched many different sites all over the country, and this was a common element in all of their regulations. I realize that since the early twenty-first century, this "hobby" of ghost hunting has become more popular and the discussions have been more open, but how is it that these two particular rules were so common in all of these sites?

The events of this made me reflect on the incident back in 1979. I was inexperienced in ghost hunting but here two times I have had tons of activity. I always hear about those who do this paranormal hunting, they go searching hundreds of times and never have any activity. Was I just lucky? Was I sensitive to the spirit world? Was I supposed to investigate these possibilities? Were these experiences related to Katie still missing? If she was in the spirit world, wouldn't she be trying to connect with me and really cuss me out? I wanted more.

# CHAPTER 15

It has been five years since my first experience at Villisca and I have become more and more active in the weekend and summer investigations. I have traveled to different states, made connections to many people that have had televised investigations. I have no interest in being on T.V., but they have the ability to grant me access to the sites that the general ghost hunting population would not be able to do. The really popular sites, such as the Ohio State Reformatory Prison, have affordable nights where you can stay and investigate the entire building, cellar to attic, but you are with one hundred other people. It is my experience that the more people there are with you, the less activity you can record or sense. I often thought that it would only be your mind playing tricks on you but when I have caught things on camera and other recording devices, my mind isn't that powerful to manipulate electronics.

There was an old library in Michigan that we spent a couple of nights in. This library was over 150 years old and a prison was on the site prior to the library. There was so much activity it was mind blowing. I was in the basement and in one corner, there was a crawl space under the oldest part of the building. My EMF meter was spiking as I got closer to this area. I had my friend, Kelly, with me. We crawled into the area and I turned on my spirit box. As the static was strong, four voices came through. Men and women were both trying to speak. One woman came through and it sounded like, "Beware."

I asked, "Beware of what? Are we in danger?"

There was a response that was another woman, but it didn't sound like the first woman. Her words sounded like, "Evil. Get out." These didn't come across as frantic or demanding but more like someone is whispering you a warning, so the bad guy didn't hear you.

I asked, "Is there something else here that would want to hurt people?" I worded it this way because I was starting to freak out but asking it in a way of not making the question personal helped me cope at that moment. Kelly was gasping. The air was cold, but we were under the building.

A man's voice comes through, a very deep and masculine voice, "Symbol, identify." I looked at Kelly, we had the same expression on our faces. When you are talking about evil and symbols, you tend to think of pentagrams or other drawn characters that are representative of a cult or religion.

We started to look around this crawl space. It was not very large, dirt floor, brick, and stone walls around the opening that we crawled through, but the other three walls were wooded, or appeared so. We could not stand up all the way, so it was easier to crawl on our hands and knees. We had flashlights and night vision cameras documenting everything for our records. I told Kelly to start examining the walls, ceiling, and floor to see if there are any types of symbols carved or drawn on any surface. It was very difficult, it was cold, dark, flashlights and night-vision were not good enough to do a confident examination of what might be supernatural or churning up some bad juju.

I told Kelly that we need different tools to know for sure, something is stirring up some crazy evidence and based on the words, there has to be something here to draw in dark energy. The organization and the library board that gave us permission to search told us what they had found in hunts before, but they were not able to stop the dark energy. They had given us seventy-two hours to investigate every inch of the library, they were closed because of a holiday weekend. We walked outside to get one of those really bright camping lanterns, hand brushed, steel brush, and a small chisel. We returned to the crawl space and set up our tools. The light made working conditions a large improvement. We started on the stone walls by brushing each stone and the grout around each one. We were wearing work gloves but when a stone was cleaned and would look like an old carving might be in the stone, I would take my hands out of the gloves, use my bare fingers to feel for a carved texture. If it would seem like there was something, I would take out thin paper and a pencil with soft lead and do a rubbing over the marks to research at a later date. Many of the rubbings were nothing but old hammer or chisel markings from one hundred-plus years ago.

This took us four hours to work the one stone wall. We kept telling ourselves to go slowly, don't assume, and I couldn't imagine how long a large wall would have taken us. By the end of the wall, it was dawn, we were tired, hungry, thirsty, and crabby. We shut everything off and decided to go to our hotel, shower, eat, and nap. I need my naps.

# Chapter 16

It was around 1:00 P.M. and we were on our way back to the library to continue to search for markings. In past hunts, it was discovered that if there are certain symbols, they can produce very powerful occurrences. I spent many years thinking that just plain drawings or words do not have the ability to bring forward magical beings or events. The more active I got with this paranormal community, I had to think about my religious upbringing. I was raised Methodist but converted to Catholic. When 9/11 happened, I got very curious about different world religions. There are more similarities and many teachings than differences if you look at the foundation. But even with the radical fundamentalists, every religion has very powerful symbols, powerful words, and prayer. If you look at miracles of religions, they are a transformation of something magical, for the lack of a better word. When you are suffering, you pray, be thankful, pray, be scared, pray, angry, pray. So, I thought, why would the right formula of symbols and words have powerful ability. If good can come from this, the opposite and equal force should be possible.

These thoughts made my paranormal investigations be much more productive and serving a bigger purpose than just thrills of finding evidence. (experience of cleaning a home)

Kelly and I got back to the crawl space and had better light, Wi-Fi accessibility and I brought my notes and written resources from my research and experience. We found many more symbols than I ever imagined. My first thought was that people had been gaining access to just do a warped paranormal type graffiti. There is so much evidence of people, Hollywood, or just plain idiots drawing symbols and have no idea if there was any such meaning or (scary thought) power. I was actually impressed with myself for the majority of the symbols I had seen and researched meanings. There is so much misunderstanding to what original purposes were behind these symbols that too often they are misused. One example is the swastika. It has been used for over three thousand years for the meaning of "good" or "to be." Hitler changed that theory. There are many other designs also. We photographed all of the symbols. I took dirt samples to run analysis on. One of the elements I was looking for was sulphur. There are so many urban legends of sulphur being a by-product of demons that I have started documenting a presence at the haunts I get to investigate. The legends of this specific building are also a concern. Even though I always tell my students that gossip or rumors are 90 percent false, we know that the 10 percent of truth could be deadly.

We gathered all of our equipment after spending seventy-two hours documenting photos, digital recordings, EVP readings, temperature changes, and historical documents of deaths or unexplained true occurrences in and around that area of the library. The drive back to Iowa was full of retelling of the weekend's adventures, our thoughts and ideas of true stories or fantasies at this time. Normally on a drive of this length, we take turns between sleeping and driving but there was so much activity that we were pumped. This is similar to the first ever haunt in Villisca. We were so full of adrenaline that we were not sleepy.

The ladies that go with me on these investigations enjoy the thrill of the unknown we are walking into, but the hours after I like to do alone. I have my own style of going through everything and I always document and share my findings or lack of findings.

One of the EVP sessions was a woman and it sounded like, "Watch out!" in an aggressive tone. There was a whisper saying, "Burn in hell." It definitely was not the same voice. There were actually thirty-two different spots in the recordings that there were disembodied voices but could not make out exactly what they were saying. There were twelve instances of the tones sounding scared or trying to warn someone. It was impossible to decipher what. I played these sounds for many people. I even bought a special computer to slow down the recording to see if I could make out the words. They were definitely fearful messages. I was a couple states away from the site and I started to get fearful. I normally have a little anxiety while investigating, but these voices were very high on the creep meter.

There were six instances of something I had never come across. I actually jumped out of my chair when I heard these. I couldn't believe my ears. There were exactly six different growls. They were not the faint growls you would see on the ghost hunting reality T.V. shows, these were inhuman and pissed. A vision would pop into my head of a mouth with sharp blood stained teeth and drool dripping down as it got close to your neck.

I wrote down the place and time of these growls, so I could go to video and still shots. The noise was so angry and threatening sounding that I couldn't imagine something not materializing.

I went to the first one. It was in the break room where there was a small kitchenette facility for the employees. The history said it was once a servant's quarters. The building was built in the early 1800s as a mansion of a lumber and railway tycoon. Michigan was not a slave state, but the historical documents were not very complimentary of the owner of the house. He was very wealthy, married only because of social demands. There were letters from his servants talking about how he would force his wife to be locked up in her bedroom while he was gone. She was only allowed to come out when there were guests, or they were going to church. I guess it was lucky for her that due to his position in the community, consistent church going was a requirement. At least she would get out on Sundays.

One letter talked about how she would be treated so badly, but he never hit her. He didn't waste time on her. He would use the female servants to communicate to her when they were going out and he would pick the clothes out. The clothes closet was in another room.

There was one servant that was from Haiti. This woman was hired, or bought, by the owner while in Florida. The owner was rumored to want to engage in some supernatural practices. This woman he brought back was a woman of color and according to herself, was a priestess in the Vodou religion. The actual term for her is Mambo. The actual religion is a belief in a supreme God, Bondye, and a lesser loa are compared to saints in the Catholic church. There is a strong belief in morality, community spirit, and giving to the poor. The vices of greed and dishonor are against the teachings.

As with every aspect of society, there is a dark presence in the Haitian Vodou as with anything else. The servant practiced dark magic. She turned the religion of loving teachings into a greedy and powerful evil. This, according to letters from other servants, excited the owner. He was in Florida at a meeting and he was introduced to her by another tycoon in the railway. The story says that she was able to make an entity appear before him and propose wealth beyond his wildest dreams if he were to take this Mambo home. The terms were that she would be treated as an aristocrat and there would be a temple in his house where she could perform rituals.

This was 1832, so the thought of trickery was not as suspicious as it is today. but he quickly came under her spell. He came home, the riches were coming in faster than ever. The strange thing was that he conducted business in his house now 80 percent of the time instead of going to the office. Many people of the community thought that maybe he was staying to care for his wife. They thought surely, she must be sick since they never see her out with him anymore nor do they attend the Lutheran church anymore.

The wife was still alive, although still a prisoner. The Haitian woman became more and more powerful. She started acting like the mistress of the house. She was barking orders to everyone. The owner became more and more submissive to the woman and more and more vicious to his wife.

There were several times that the other servants, according to journals, the owner and the Haitian woman would have sex, very loud and aggressive sex. They did not try to hide it. It was always up in the attic.

After it had been five years, the staff hired a new upstairs house maid. The first day was very busy and the Mistress of the house was out. The experienced maids and butler didn't take time to explain the do's and don'ts for the upstairs. She knew her job was to keep the second floor in order and clean. She opened a door thinking it might be a closet, but it was a door to stairs. It was obvious leading to the attic. One thing they did tell her was never to go up there. The door was always locked, and so this surprised her to find it unlocked. She poked her head in the stairwell and listened for noises to see if someone was up there. There was no sound. She started to sniff, smelling something. She had grown up on a farm that did its own butchering. She was familiar with the smell of death and rotted flesh. This smell from the attic was a smell she had known. It was a mixture of dirt, wax, and death. She started to take a step on the first step when the head maid slammed the door shut. The head maid told her that if she wanted to continue to earn money and keep on living, she will never poke her head in that area again. There is something not right up there and it will do a body good to stay away.

There had been four weeks go by and the new maid stayed away from the attic. Her quarters were on the main floor in the back of the house but at any time the Mistress wanted something, the new girl would have to comply. Many of the requests were very strange. Some of them were, have a cart of whisky outside the attic door, bring up a crate of live chickens, have black undergarments for women cleaned, folded, and placed outside the door. There were always candles being bought and placed outside the door.

The owner of the mansion would be led upstairs every night by the Haitian Mistress. The people in the household could hear screaming, yelling, and moaning. There were many snickers among the servants of a rough sex life. The stories many made up were fantastic and difficult for the younger servants to imagine. The new maid was only sixteen, a virgin, and had no sexual experience other than seeing two dogs mating.

One of the married couples that worked and lived at the mansion had three, young children. They were two boys: fifteen and twelve, and one girl, ten. They helped out in small ways whenever they were not in school. These were very quiet and obedient children. After the Mistress became more powerful in the dealings with the house, she would have the oldest boy come up to the attic with her. The new maid questioned him when they were outside and asked why he was going up to the attic. Nothing but evil goes on up there. Several commandments were being broken every night. He said that she promised him that she would pay for him to go to the university if he did some chores for her. He wanted to get away from this place so badly, get a career and get his family out of here. The promise of money is a very powerful type of magic itself.

The boy became very withdrawn after five days of this new responsibility. His color of his skin almost had a greenish tint to it, like he was the walking dead. He didn't speak to anyone anymore other than one word answers. When he was away from the house, his family and friends were asking what was wrong, was he being abused by the Mistress or the owner? He would never reply to that question. He looked like he was in a trance.

One day, it was time to get up and do the morning chores, it was summer, so the kids were all available to help. The oldest boy did not report to the kitchen when everyone ate breakfast together before the household woke up. They went to his room that he shared with his siblings and there was no sign of him. His brother and sister were sleeping so soundly that they had no idea if he ever came to bed or not.

This started a search immediately around the grounds. No horses or buggies were missing. His clothes were still in the room. The owner woke up and started screaming at everyone as to why breakfast for him and the Mistress had not been ready. The mother and father of the boy explained what had happened and that they were worried about the missing boy. The Mistress and the owner didn't act surprised at all. They mentioned how he was doing extra chores in order to pay for the university. He had said he hated it here, so maybe he just decided to leave early.

The parents disagreed with them, they said he had not finished high school yet, he didn't have any money yet, that didn't make sense.

This display of standing firm did not go over well. They were told that if they were so concerned, they could pack up and go look for the boy full time. Of course, the parents knew they couldn't do that since they had other children to take care of. They needed the owner's horses in order to get to town.

The new maid witnessed this all going down. She didn't believe that the boy left on his own. The first chance she would get, she was going up to the attic to investigate. She knew he must be up there against his will or sick.

Quite a bit of time had gone by and she didn't get to sneak up stairs. The new maid and other servants would get taken to town in a wagon twice a month to get personal items for themselves and to do the shopping for the household. Whenever a group of women get together, which many servants from other homes would meet in town at the same time, would gossip and talk about local news. Every time there was news about more people going missing. This was in the 1800s, so people missing without telling anyone wasn't so strange, but the fact so many incidents were happening and so many across socio-economic statuses and races that it was never connected until the tenth person in one month disappeared.

The laborers that went missing were employees of friends of the owner of the mansion that this story originated from. It seemed that the employers of the missing people would all of a sudden get very rich in a matter of days. Bad news would be followed by great fortune. I would think if I had received great fortune, I would smile a lot. According to the diary, these people turned very, very mean and would not be out socializing anymore.

There were three wives of three different wealthy men of the area that went missing also. This is what started the local sheriff's department to start looking into the events. The families always seemed to be very happy, giving, and pillar of the community. When no one in their family would even talk about where they women might have gone or why, many evil rumors started floating around.

One thing that all of these had in common was that those men of the different businesses and households would be visiting the mansion more and more. They would start in the man's office but always end up in the attic following the Haitian Priestess. The new maid would be spying on them more and more, still trying to find a time to sneak up there to look around.

There was a symbol showing up all over town on the walls of the houses and buildings where someone had gone missing. It was the same symbol, and it would have gone unnoticed except that when the new maid and the head maid were walking down the street, they noticed it and mentioned to each other that symbol had been on the door to the attic as well. One day the new maid had to run to town to pick up some packages that were mailed from Miami, Florida. One of the male servants, an older, grandpa-like person, drove her on the buggy to get the items. They got to share the stories with each other, and she told him of what she had discovered. She asked him if he would drive the horses around to see if that symbol had been on all of the other houses or buildings. He agreed, he said he wanted to prove to her that her creative mind was getting carried away.

They got to town and there were ten different sites to visit. This community wasn't very large, so addresses were well known. With each building they drove by, they kept hoping there was no sign of the symbol. This time of our history, superstition was very strong. The belief in evil is what kept people in church.

They approached the first building, looked very closely at the front. No sign was observed. They looked at each other and both grinned and had a deep sigh. The thought that maybe that the Haitian priestess was just getting involved in the rich men as a prostitute and the wives had enough and left their husbands. It didn't explain the other seven people missing, but perhaps they were just super religious, and they couldn't stomach the men cheating so openly. Anyway, they felt relieved and decided to go uptown to do their errands and get back home.

The older man snapped the reins of the horses to proceed in front of the house, but the horses shook, screamed, reared up, and refused to walk in front of the house. The man got off of the buggy to check and see if something got in one of their hooves, or a piece of the harness was harming them. He couldn't find anything. He decided to take hold of the reins and lead them on foot. The horses reacted violently, knocked the man down and ran off. While they started to run, he yelled for the new maid to jump off. She leaped off onto the grass yard next to them. They watched the horses run across the yards and did not run down the road in front of the house.

She ran to check on the old man, no broken bones but was a little bruised and sore. He couldn't understand what got into them, crazy fools. He said it looked like they were running toward Main Street, so he said to go through the yard and cut through the alley to try to find the horses and buggy. They walked by the side of the house they were looking at and for some reason, the temperature got very cold. They were in the shade on the side of the house so naturally they didn't give it another thought since they were really worried about the horses.

The old man stopped in his tracks and started to feel like he was going to throw up. He bent over, putting his hands on his knees. The girl felt sick too, not as violently as the older man. She didn't know if he was going to make it, so she looked up to the house to see if anyone was looking out the windows, so she could get some help. As she looked up, her eyes bugged out, her mouth gaped open in shock. There was the same symbol as the one at their house on the attic door. The cross with the infinity symbol under it. There were two horizontal lines on the vertical line. Looking at it makes her light-headed. She grabbed the arm of the older man and yelled at him to look! He stared at the symbol; it was obvious to the wiser gentleman that this was dark magic, evil. He yelled at the girl to help him get away from the house. He leaned on her shoulders and they struggled to get away. The farther they walked the better they felt. The strain of the negative energy caused them both to sit on the road behind the house, in the alley. Recovering was needed before they could go any further. As they sat there, panting, catching their breath and allowing their heart rate to slow down, they noticed something that escaped them from the front. The houses next to the affected one were vacant. This was a very affluent neighborhood; this did not happen. The houses were the same age as the affected house, but they looked hundred years older and looked like they were abandoned for decades. They know for sure that was not true.

The old man told the young girl, that symbol was the work of the devil and they had to get their family and leave the mansion immediately. He said that was why the horses were acting like that, animals have more sense in feeling evil than humans do.

Once the two recovered and could continue, they found the horses at the livery stable. The man who owned it was teasing the old man. They knew each other very well, so he acted like he could get a laugh out of the old man. The tension was obvious, the owner asked them if they were okay. The old man responded that they were fine, just a family emergency happened, so they had to leave.

The new maid was voicing her concern about not having transportation nor money to leave. She was not related to anyone at the house, so she knew she would be on her own. He told her to come with them. They could camp at night, travel by day. They would find work somewhere, but they had to leave.

The two got back to the main house as fast as the horses could run. The old man was sweating and acting very scared. He grabbed the young maid by her shoulders and in a forceful whisper, he told her to get to the house, tell the others to grab just enough belongings that they could carry on their back and get to the barn in twenty minutes. He was planning on unharnessing the horses and letting off of the animals loose, so the owners or foremen could not run and look for the servants for a while. He was also getting nervous because it was late enough in the day that the dinner and chore hour was fast approaching.

The young maid ran as fast as she could, she commanded the young children playing outside to come with her. She picked up the youngest one because the child would have been too slow. She shared the information with the oldest female servant since she was the leader. This woman was amazing. Since she used to be a slave, she had taught all of the others to always have a travel bag ready to go just in case they needed to escape quickly. She always thought the reason would be slave owners and not the supernatural evil in the world. The women and children were almost ready in just a few minutes. They knew better than to all run to the barn at once, so just a few at a time went just in case one of the owners would see them.

The young maid had to go up to the top floor just under the attic to her room. She only had three dresses, two undergarments and she was wearing her only pair of shoes. She threw open the door and put her belongings on top of a bed sheet, drew the corners together to use it as a bag. She started out of the room and had to run past the door to the attic on her way to the back staircase. She was trying to be as quiet as possible as she went by and faintly, she heard her name being called by what sounded like a young boy. She thought it was the missing boy. He cried out for help: "Help me, please, I can't get out!" He was sobbing uncontrollably. The young girl stopped dead in her tracks, she was sweating and frozen at the same time. Her desire to get out and to help him was fighting her body to move. Once she looked around and saw that she was alone, she slowly and quietly turned the doorknob to the attic. It made just the faintest metal on metal scraping sound. She leaned in and saw the wooden narrow stairs going up in the dark.

The young girl called out to the boy, "Are you up here?" Time went by and all she could hear was whimpering. As her eyes adjusted to the dark, it seemed there was either a candle burning or sunlight bleeding through the cracks in the ceiling.

As the boy's cries continued, she knew she had to try to rescue him. She knew the Haitian Priestess and the owner was not at home, so she felt this was the best time. He would be able to escape with the rest of them.

Every step up the stairs was made carefully and with caution. The wood groaned with each step. The smell was becoming more and more pungent. If anyone could smell death this was it. She had to put her hand over her nose, if the boy was up here, the smell had to be causing him harm. She got up to the top of the steps, the landing turned to the left before she could see anything. At the far end of the small attic, there were hundreds of candles burning. It seemed to be an altar, like the wooden ones the other servants constructed in the barn for Sunday services. There were dried flowers hanging from the rafters, the ceiling was covered in them.

At the bottom of the altar, was a mound of dirt. Over the mound, on a piece of wood was a symbol burned into the wood. It was the same symbol as the ones in the town. It looked like compass arrows and extra lines on the vertical lines. The sweat was beading and running down the girl's face, but she was freezing. She bent over the mound and she couldn't take her eyes away from this. The dirt appeared to be breathing. In her mind it had to be an animal buried alive under the dirt. It was not that big, so she thought of a cat or dog. She slowly moved her hands to the dirt to uncover whatever was breathing, she wanted to save its life. As she started to dig with her hands, she noticed the dirt was wet and cold.

In a blink of an eye, a small hand burst up through the dirt and grabbed her hand. She screamed and tried to pull away. While her and the hand were pulling on each other, the dirt fell away from a face. It was the young boy. His eyes were wide with terror. He opened his mouth and nothing, but mud flowed out. He blinked, she screamed, and these huge tentacles sprung out and wrapped around the girl. They wrapped around her forehead, legs, and waist.

From behind, she heard the voice of the Priestess. She was chanting some strange language. Their eyes locked and the Priestess declared the sacrifices being made to keep her powerful and to have the riches from the community under her control. The younger the sacrifices, the happier the demon was. She was not a Priestess; she was a witch. The tentacles squeezed and as they pulled the girl down into the dirt, they folded her in half backwards.

# Chapter 17

This story is embedded in my mind. That symbol seems very familiar but after all the sites I have visited from haunted sites here in the United States to many ruins all over the world, it is very likely I have seen it before but never investigated it. The hundreds of horror movies bad and decent also could use many generic or accidently real symbols.

I researched this symbol more, I needed to know why and how to stop the power. Why hunt all these supernatural events without knowing how to help people!

I didn't have the ability to travel to Haiti but there is a lot of information on the internet and library, so my knowledge is only from literature. The symbol seems to have originated from the 1700s when many ships were trapping people for slave ships. The lore states that a strong Medicine Man from a village in Haiti witnessed many of his family captured and dragged to a ship. It is unknown if it was from the New World or England, but it was terrifying and made this powerful Medicine Man angry.

He had tapped into a power that had seemed like a blessing, but it was evil mimicking as blessing. He started a prayer to give him strength. There was chanting and smoke. The smoke took the shape of a creature that spoke to him. This voice granted him power as long as his body was led to the marked spot, alive, the man would experience his greatest wishes. As the smoke cleared, it left behind the mark. The document's crude drawing looked just like the one in the diary of the maid's and the one in the basement of the library in Michigan.

After further research, trying to uncover lore of how to stop the power I did not uncover any information. I documented the knowledge I found, backed it up to the "cloud" and moved on.

# Chapter 18

I was back at work at my high school. Day to day dealing with tardiness, truancy, students disrespecting teachers, vaping in the bathroom, meetings, and daily documentation. The one thing I loved about going to work was the practical jokes we all would play on each other. Students would see us laugh and have harmless fun.

There was always a small group of students that tried to act "gangsta" when they were at school. This always made me chuckle due to the fact the biggest buildings in our area were corn bins. This was 100 percent farm country. It was obvious that teens sometimes due to the environment they like to test their power or independence but sometimes they just try to be powerful in ways that don't fit. They have never scared me; I think of the supernatural things I have experienced or researched, and these teens have nothing on the supernatural. I always thought it would be interesting to take the rebellious teens on one of these hunts and see their courage then.

They think I fake not being scared of them, but I don't. After all these years dealing with troubled teens, and the more I get into trying to clean haunting sites, I get bored with real people.

# CHAPTER 19

In October that year, I was invited to come to my old high school's fortieth class reunion. I was expecting this. I was dreading this. I hate the fact that I have aged. I must have been the only one to have aged in forty years. I am ridiculous but vanity speaks to one's mind like that sometimes.

Usually our reunions are in the summer, but our school wants to honor certain classes during our Homecoming game which is always in September or October. I checked the date, and it happens to be on the same weekend as the Homecoming at the school that employs me. I always have to attend the home games for supervision and the dance the next night for supervision. I like the games, but dances are not fun. The school I work at has really never had behavior problems at dances. I decided to see if I could get out of supervising the dance because I need to attend my homecoming as honored alumni. My principal agreed I could miss the dance. The principal was very involved in the Alumni organization of the school where I work, so he was very supportive of me attending the entire weekend. I was allowed to skip out of the supervision duties this weekend.

If anyone believes in signs, I guess this was a powerful one. I got home, sent in my RSVP, and dug out my old yearbook. The more I looked through old photos the more I was happy about the decision to attend.

That Friday showed up and I went to work. On the day of the Homecoming game, classes are only thirty minutes long, lunch is a sack lunch outside around the football stadium. They have class games, then at one-fifteen, high school is dismissed. The homecoming parade is at two o'clock. By three o'clock, the parade is over, busses have picked everyone up, I hang around for forty-five minutes more in case someone needs help. By four o'clock, I have my bags packed and I am in my car heading to my hometown. I have satellite radio, so I play songs from my high school years to get in the mood.

# Chapter 20

I got to my hometown by six o'clock that evening. I couldn't stay at my parents' home anymore since they weren't around anymore. I knew that I could get a hotel room twenty miles away but if I was going to go drinking, part of our class culture, I didn't want to drive. Everything in that town was walking distance. There was a former funeral home that was a large Victorian style house. The granddaughter of the funeral director bought the house and remodeled it into a B&B. It was beautiful and the fact it was in an old funeral home was right up my alley.

I had not shared with any of my old classmates from my weekend/summer job, but it was common knowledge by now. When I started, it was laughed about, but due to reality shows on T.V. it was accepted more. Plus, with my more mature age, I didn't give a shit if they laughed or not. I have learned to laugh at myself.

I checked in at the B&B, changed my clothes to more appropriate Autumn football gear and decided to walk to the field. The B&B was in the middle of town, the field was at the far north of town. It would only take five minutes if that to get there.

I got to the gate to pay for the game, and recognized 90 percent of the people going in. I couldn't remember names for the life of me, but I did remember their faces. They seemed to remember my name.

I had to fake it until I heard someone call them by name or it came to me. I have lots of practice with this at my job. Students who never get in trouble come talk to me. It is obvious that they would know my name, but I don't want to offend them that I don't remember their name, so I excused myself, whispered to my secretary (she knows all of them due to registration) and then I came back. I hope no one ever figured that anyone knew what I was doing.

There was a section of the bleachers reserved for the Class of 1979. It was way too large, there were only thirty-three of us, four have passed away, and they never all show up. But, maybe with spouses and children, we could use half of the space. I knew I was being negative. It is strange how you can be out of high school (as a student) for forty years but still have the same insecurities as an eighteen-year-old. Would anyone talk to me? Will I look old and wrinkly more than anyone else? Will people judge me because my marriage to the town's bad boy failed? UGH

People started filling in, names were coming back to me and in a short time, those stupid thoughts and fears vanished from my head. Just like in high school, the girls and boys segregated, although the conversation between the two groups was more fun and easier.

The game started, I love football, but we were talking way too much. It was halftime and I had not caught up on all the gossip yet. We were laughing, teasing, reminiscing, and enjoying the night immensely. No pressure, acceptance for just being there.

The game was over, we won, but they always won since they switched to eight-man football. The local bar was where we all went afterwards. I got a ride with someone and we went in to push tables together. The bartender knew our names and I actually remembered hers as well. She was working at the bar thirty-plus years ago. I think she owned it.

We got to talking and the subject of the shows of ghost hunting came up. I had a few beers in me, and so I started to share my start of ghost hunting several years ago. I was actually surprised and happy at the reactions of my friends. They were interested, no chuckling, asking questions. I started talking about the contacts I have made, how I have worked with a few of the T.V. personalities from a few ghost hunting shows. The research I have conducted in old cellars, attics, ruins in Mexico, England, Greece, and Italy. The information collected from the Catholic Church archives.

This discussion leads to death talk. Then it turns a corner about the classmates that we have lost. Someone brought up the name, Katie. The game Lost Trail was brought up. We discussed the disappearance of Katie being the last time we ever played that game. No one, me included, put a connection of Lost Trail and Katie's disappearance together other than the date.

I asked a couple of the girls who still live in the area about Katie's family. They said they didn't know, they never saw them, and didn't know when or where they had left town.

The topic flowed to the subject of Lost Trail. We started talking about how over the years and contacts that others have made, we have never met anyone else who had played something like that. This information made all of us feel special.

A suggestion was made to play it this weekend. I enthusiastically said YES! The guys have never played this game and honestly, we didn't invite them. All of the girls agreed except for the women who were married into the class. They said they would hold down the fort at the country club while we were out scaring each other. They would pick us up if we couldn't make the run across town anymore. I laughed; running is funny.

It was agreed upon, Saturday night, after the dinner, we would start playing Lost Trail again. The country club was a rather small building that had a large dining area connected to a kitchen facility. Many of the people like to play golf before we start the dinner. This was the perfect place; it was on the far north side of town, so we would just start there. It was cold enough not to get sweaty and the mosquitoes would not be out. Everyone was told to bring chalk and flashlights. I am glad I came to this.

# CHAPTER 21

I spent the night at the bed and breakfast. I was very curious, given my weekend hobby of ghost hunting if I would sense anything in this converted funeral home. I had my equipment in my car, and I thought I would not want to get it out, but I couldn't resist. I set it up in my room only. I didn't want to freak people out who were staying here also. It was only two other couples, but I was thinking that they would freak out about me more than what I was doing.

I set up my SLS camera, my rem pod and digital recorder. My mind was on high alert, surely something would be present. This building was a funeral home for four decades. I stayed awake until 3:00 A.M. trying to coax some presence, record something, but it was quiet. I shut everything off, went to sleep.

I slept very soundly, which is unusual for me. The beer, reconnecting with old friends, and trying to find spirits in my room did relax me. My Uncle and his son (my cousin) were the Sheriff and Deputy of our county. I have always said I wanted to be a police officer since third grade. They had let me do ride-alongs when I was in high school. But the closest thing to a cop was being an administrator in a high school.

Since my hometown was so very small, my Uncle knew I was going to be in town for the reunion. There is no getting around this community in secret. Social media had nothing on small towns. I had asked him if he would mind picking me up and driving me around the town and rural areas to catch up on changes.

He picked me up at 8:00 A.M. on Saturday morning. I woke up at 7:45 A.M. Luckily, I had brought a hat, slapped on some deodorant, threw on some sweats, a hoodie and made it out to the patrol car on time. He said he needed to drive to a nearby community to deliver some papers to a farmer, so we went out to the country first before driving around the town. During the ride, which the farmer lived only fifteen miles outside of Lenox, we talked about current events in our personal lives. I talked about my job at the school, he talked about the law enforcement duties in rural Iowa. I remember riding along in the seventies, in the middle of the night, struggling to stay awake. Not much action, no cow tipping or outhouse burning or anything. The biggest difference from 1979 to 2019 was the meth houses. Since the eighties farm crisis, many old houses out in the middle of nowhere have gone abandoned. It is amazing how these drug dealers can sniff out these properties.

I filled him in on all of my travels. I didn't think he would think anything about it. I figured I would get teased; he had a vicious sense of humor. But he asked if my travels were work or pleasure and since he knew I was divorced, he asked if I traveled alone. I thought about making up a semi-truth, but decided, what the hell, I told him every-thing about my hobby/ pseudo- expert ghost hunting. I always felt a little separated from my cousins, or never taken seriously, so I pre-pared myself for an embarrassing reaction. It didn't happen.

He asked tons of questions. I talked about equipment research, the amount of time I spend researching the history of sites, and the amount of time I spend reviewing all of the data. I explained the re-search of Catholic exorcism rites and lore of spirits and incantations. I surprised myself at how much I talked and surprised at the total at-tention he was paying to my words.

He was asking about some of my war stories of some of the ghost explorations and it is always fun to share these. I talked about several, but it is always fun to talk about the amazing data collected from the murder house in Villisca, which is only twenty miles from Lenox.

I talked about the last project I worked on in Michigan in the old library. I talked about the symbols we discovered under the building and the origin of Haiti. The stories of missing people occurring in the area wherever the symbols occurred. I explained the lore I discovered about the origin of the symbols being connected with demon summoning, sacrificing people, and the amount of power the people gain after the victims went missing. My cousin was driving his patrol car listening to me, mouth open, speechless. The conversation changed to "Do you believe all of this?" I explained that I approach every hunt with a plan to debunk claims, and there have been some that I feel have been debunked. The exciting part is when all attempts to debunk fail, and I have data that no science or rational explanation can explain, I get an adrenaline rush. I have been fortunate enough to have established a reputation with some of the reality T.V. ghost hunters and have had meetings with them either in person or face time. That won him over big time.

We moved on from this conversation and he asked about who all returned for the class reunion. The fact that there were only thirty-three people in my class, and we had over twenty show up, that is amazing. He couldn't remember who all was in my class and I reminded him of Katie being in my class. The Katie who disappeared during our Lost Trail game. He was just starting out in the Sheriff's department that year. One does not forget a case like that. I talked about our traditional Lost Trail and how we were "forced" to have her at my party. My cousin knew my dad very well, so he understood how that happened.

I asked him about what the scene looked like, what evidence was there, and who were the main suspects? We heard rumors of all of this forty years ago but nothing specific or from officials. He looked concerned, he could get in trouble showing the crime scene photos, but it was an extremely cold case. I used my "sweet—I got what I wanted" voice and explained some of the gruesome information I had uncovered at my paranormal investigations. "Look at it this way...I was with her that night. I really never got questioned, so you could say you are trying out new leads," I said.

He responded, "Okay, I would like to talk to you about it myself. I didn't know her, I knew or had met some of the family members, but since I was so new at this job, I didn't really get to be part of the discussion. What the hell? I am retiring anyway; let's go to the station house."

We got to the station house and went into the records room. I was surprised to see it was transferred to digital. "When did forty-year-old records make it to the cloud?"

He told me that unsolved crimes, especially felonies, were digitized first for preservation of data and photos. Any physical evidence such as clothing, or actual items were still kept until there was an arrest.

We sat down at his desk and he pulled up the file with the description of the scene. Then I looked at the photos.

The investigations of my paranormal sites such as ones with a gruesome history have never caused me to get squeamish. The documents and photos of what we were looking at were old, history of no connection to me, but the photos of the scene of Katie getting murdered was too close to home. I actually felt like vomiting. This feeling makes me very angry since I always quietly felt people who vomited were weak, ridiculous. Here I was, feeling weak and ridiculous.

The old house was the one next to my late grandparents' house. I remember my cousins and I at Grandma's playing dress up or something young girls played before the internet or cable T.V. We would be running up and down the sidewalk on the block and go up to the abandoned house's front porch because there was an old porch swing. We would sit on the swing going back and forth quite fast and would even hit the house several times when we swing back.

I remember we would stop and be talking, there would be a noise coming from the house. We would freeze, look at each other. "Did you hear someone at the door?" I would ask.

Roseanne, Kim, or Kelly (anyone of them) would say something like, "It sounded like someone walking."

"I didn't think anyone lived here!" I would say. None did, I remember an elderly lady lived there but passed away several years ago. Grandma and Grandpa would say that she was a miser. She has lots and lots of money, was very rude to everyone, and died a miserable woman. No one knew where her money came from, but it kept rolling in.

I had never been inside of the house, so these photos were my first exposure to the interior. There was a shot of the living room, spots where the dust had been disturbed. My cousin said they think Katie sat there hiding for some time. This statement bothered me; she was hiding because of Lost Trail. I am impressed she was brave enough to hide in there. She played the game like a pro, none of us would have ever done that.

I then looked at the photos of the kitchen. I was confused. "What is that? Is that blood or mud? Is that a hole in the floor?"

He said, "The main substance inside and on the edges of the hole was dry dirt and wet mixed in with blood. They took samples from seventy-five different areas all over the kitchen, and it was all the same—Katie's."

I then saw the next photo of the entire kitchen, even though it was a very small kitchen, the amount of blood all over the cupboards, walls, even the ceiling was shocking. It looked like someone had a garden hose and instead of shooting out water, they shot out blood all over the room.

The retching feeling came again. I asked to see photos of Katie. He said, "They never found the body."

I looked at him, we had a funeral since we were still in school and she was a classmate. He reminded me that there was a memorial service for her at the school gym but that there was no coffin. I reminded him that there is a headstone at the cemetery. He explained that it is common for people to put headstones when a loved one is missing in order to have a public display of remembering.

"How do we know she was murdered?" I asked.

He looked at me like I was a little sister trying to pester my older brother and our cousin. "What?" I exclaimed. I hated that look.

He said that the amount of blood in the room would have drained her entire body. It would be impossible for anyone to live with that amount of blood loss.

This was before DNA tests, etc. What other evidence was there that proved this was Katie? He brought out a box with some physical evidence in it. He pulled out shreds of clothing that was hers. There were strands of black hair with pieces of scalp attached.

I asked to look at the photos again and he let me sit at the desk as he took care of some phone calls. I felt like the photo of the hole needed some more examination, just a woman's intuition. When my cousin got off the phone, I asked him how deep was the hole? One would expect the body to be at the bottom of it.

He said that it was over fifty feet. They had to call in some engineers from the State Department to figure out what this was. They wrote some report of an old well under that house, pressure had built up over the decades and as Katie walked over the spot, it exploded, cutting her up and she fell into the hole. It was so deep that recovery was impossible. This was the "theory." It was a stupid theory, there has never been any documentation of anything happening like this anywhere in the Midwest. They were trying to put an end to the investigation since they had absolutely no idea of what happened. There were no footprints going out of the house, none of the exterior was bothered, no blood residue outside, they were out of leads.

I looked up the photo of the hole and printed it off, so I could take it with me. There were strange markings on the floor and another four symbols on walls around the hold as if they were marking north, east, south, and west. These markings looked familiar; I knew I had seen them before. My mind was racing with too many thoughts, so I couldn't remember.

I had asked about the old lady that owned the property. He had the name and that there was a great-great nephew and niece somewhere in Florida. Their family has very strong legal instructions ever since the old lady was alive that the property would never be sold. I questioned him about this because the house had been empty since 1972, why would anyone want an old house that was falling apart stay up. I would think it would be a safety hazard.

My cousin responded to me saying that the family has it securely updated just so it doesn't fall. They have instructions of never stepping foot inside, they are just to check the roof and foundation from the outside and make it secure. They were multi-millionaires, so they didn't need to sell it for income. Wow, I didn't get it. None of the family had lived in Lenox since the old lady died.

# Chapter 22

My cousin had to take me back to the B&B. It was around two o'clock by then, and I was starving. I went to the Tiger Den, the burger and ice cream shop in town. I got a sandwich, FF, and a drink and took it back to my room.

I couldn't get those symbols out of my mind. I pulled the photos that I printed from the crime scene and laid them on the bed as I was eating. My phone buzzed and I got a text from Kelli giving me some information about another investigation. I checked the calendar we have set up on Google and booked it.

It was like a lightbulb flashed in my eyes. I remembered where I had seen those symbols. This is why I have to document everything. I swear my brain leaks out my ears.

I had my equipment from my unsuccessful investigation from the night before. I pulled out my computer, got on the Wi-Fi and brought up my report and photos of the investigation from the library in Michigan. I re-read the information of the powerful people from Haiti and the priestess. I pulled up the photos of Kelli and I looked under the ground of the library and found it. The symbols there were exactly like the ones in the house Katie died in, or was mutilated in.

As I checked my notes from the origin of the activity in Michigan, the powerful demon that is controlled by the symbol, the sacrifices made and giving the person who controlled the symbol of power and wealth. I didn't realize that if the symbol was undisturbed, it would go on for generations.

The description of what the demon does to its victims was very disturbing. Most of the research I have done over the years talk about Demons controlling or possessing humans, but this one survived on the flesh and blood of people.

I researched the name of the owners and thanks to my connections in many different agencies, I am able to gain access to certain government websites that normally I would not be able to.

The name of the original lady who lived in Lenox gave me enough information to find out her husband's name and how they earned a living. I also was able to see the comings and goings from records of their passport. This was very unusual since he was a farmer, they lived in town, and it was rare for farmers to travel abroad in the forties and fifties. The husband, Ben, was in WWII and was stationed in Africa for most of it. When he was called up, he had just gotten married to sixteen-year-old, Judy. They both had grown up on a farm during the depression and Ben's dad left him sixty acres. Judy had to take care of the land, a few milk cows, and a few hogs while Ben was fighting the war. According to the timeline some broadcast companies did when they did a story on the riches of the present family, Ben and Judy were very poor. They grew their own food, made their own clothes. She was able to sell mild, pork, and some eggs to sustain her while he was gone.

While Ben was in Africa, he got separated from his squad. He was walking along the river in Egypt. He saw some locals in a small caravan. Ben was starving and he knew he was going in the right direction, but it would be many hours of walking before he reached his camp.

The people in the caravan were friendly and welcomed him into their area. They fed him and gave him a drink. He was happy to find out that one of the older women knew a decent amount of English.

She was born in Haiti and lived there until seventeen years old. She met a sailor and moved to London and lived there for several years, but Egypt was her homeland now. The sailor she married was originally from Egypt. The others in the caravan were relatives of hers. She asked Ben about him, his life, family, and life in America. It may have been the drink he had but he opened up about everything. His love, Judy, the farm, having no money, but Judy and Ben didn't complain. As long as they were healthy and able to grow their own food and pay their bills, that is all they wanted.

During this conversation, one of the young children was eating his snack of dates and started to choke. Ben had some training being in the military, but not a lot. He jumped up and picked up the child, started pounding on his back. As he held him, his left hand was holding the child just under the rib cage and the right hand was pounding his back. The food popped out of the child's mouth and started to breathe.

The entire caravan was crying, carrying on like the boy was brought back from the dead. Ben knew the boy could have died, but he felt uncomfortable from the reactions he was getting.

The old lady made a comment that Ben did not understand. She said, "Ours is not for sacrifice; you saved our boy from Ikenty." He had no idea what she was talking about.

# Chapter 23

The family wanted to show Ben their gratitude for saving one of them. He kept saying, "No, it is what anyone would do."

The old lady disagreed. She said someone like Ben should benefit from the world while he was in his physical body. Ben was afraid she meant something like sex, he didn't want to do anything against Judy.

That was not what she meant, she made Ben sit down next to the fire. A strange symbol was drawn in the dirt. The woman smeared soot on her finger and drew a symbol on Ben's forehead. She started chanting something that sounded like Latin mixed with French. Ben started to get lightheaded. He started to feel like he wanted to vomit.

A large flash happened, and a large creature was standing in the fire. It resembled an eight-foot bird, but it had a black cat's head. It was so nasty, covered in blood and screamed the most horrible scream Ben had ever heard.

Ben's head was pounding and then he passed out.

# CHAPTER 24

Ben started to wake up, his vision was blurry, and had trouble remembering the night before. Then he remembered, could see clearly, and was more scared than during battles in the war.

The old lady talked to him and explained the gratitude they had for saving the life of the young boy. To show their thanks, they put a "blessing" on Ben and his future generations. She gave him a drawing of the symbol, gave him instructions of painting it in a building or house. It must be on four walls facing north, south, east, and west. There must be a circle in the middle of the four drawings. The drawing must be done in blood, can be animal blood. Then his life will become prosperous, powerful, and will never want for anything ever again. The only thing is that once a year, he must bring a stranger to stand in the circle in the middle of the symbols. Once that person is in the circle, stand back, or leave because your blessings will be strong for you but deadly for the stranger. You cannot imagine the greatness that will unfold before you. Do not be scared of this blessing.

Ben was staring at the drawing, instructions, and the old woman. She explained how she has been blessed since she escaped from Haiti to Egypt. Her people were being slaughtered by criminals and this power saved her family and now they have riches beyond any imagination. He couldn't comprehend the magnitude of what was in his future.

Just then, he could hear engines in the distance. He recognized a convoy of jeeps coming near him. He folded the paper, thanked everyone for the food and hospitality and ran to wave down the jeeps. He got back to the camp, checked in and reported to his commander as to why he got separated.

Ben went to his bunk and began to write a long letter to Judy and explained the strange event that occurred. He put the instructions from the old lady into the envelope with his letter to Judy and mailed it. He was then sent back out on duty. As he was performing the duties of a soldier, he put the "blessing" out of his mind and struck it up to a third world superstition.

# Chapter 25

When Judy received Ben's letter, she read about the incident. She thought he had lost his mind. She laid the letter on the desk and went out to do her chores.

A few weeks went by and everything went wrong for Judy. The pigs got a condition called pseudorabies. Her small herd of sows had to be put to death. She couldn't sell them for meat. The rendering truck was the only option. Her facility was listed quarantined. It had to be empty for a minimum of three months. Her facility was wood, so it had to be treated. This was very expensive. Judy spent many nights crying. She can't afford to buy more pigs, can't afford the treatment solution for the barn; luckily, she had her milk cows.

One morning she was out in the barn milking the cows and someone drove in the yard. This always made her nervous that it would be military coming to tell her Ben had died. It was a Government vehicle but not military. The Department of Ag had driven up to her barn. They informed her that her cows would have to be slaughtered due to the pseudorabies. This disease is highly contagious and in order for the state to get a handle on it, all exposed livestock must be slaughtered. It is a state law. She told them she couldn't do that but since they were so poor, they brought their own stock trailer. They had to take the milk as well. The chickens and their eggs were all destroyed as well. Judy could only stand and watch. She didn't move for a long time. Everything she owned was being driven out of her farm to their death.

Shock is the only way to explain why Judy stood there for so long. "How am I going to live? How am I going to pay bills? What do I tell Ben? I will be homeless in a month. Ben should never have married me. I am cursed. I have $53.78 left for the rest of my life. I am such a failure. Ben would be better off without me. Did I bring this on? How long had the animals had this? Oh, my God! I am so sorry, Ben."

She fell on her knees, wept. Couldn't move, no dog to come up and give her comfort. The dogs had to be slaughtered as well.

# Chapter 26

Judy doesn't know how long she had been there, on the ground outside of her barn. She sat up; it was dark. The pain in her back and side told her she was in that spot for several hours.

She was upset she just didn't get run over or die in her sleep. She walked into the very lonely house. For the next five days, Judy laid in her bed, still in the same clothes from the day of the slaughter, as Judy called it in her mind. She would get up to get toast, water, go to the bathroom, lay back down. Judy was in a depressive trance. She would think of running away, she was too chicken to kill herself. Could she find someone to kill her? That was an idea she stuck with.

The next day, day six, there was a knock at the door. She decided that if it was the Army, she would definitely kill herself.

She got up to the door, hair was wildly sticking up and smashed on one side. Who cares about physical looks when life is over! She looked out the window and saw that it was the postman. He had a large bundle of letters, papers, etc.

The door opened and the postman said, "Hi Judy. We couldn't put any more mail in the mailbox. I figured I better come to the house to check on you. Everyone in town is pretty worried. We haven't seen you for a long time. Ben okay?"

Judy felt embarrassed. "Oh, yes, he is. I haven't been feeling well, the government took our livestock. I am quite stressed about what to do."

He responded, "We heard about the pseudorabies. Livingston's over by Clearfield had the same thing happen. It seems to be spreading. But they have a lot of land, and they will be able to bounce back."

Judy thought to herself that with only sixty acres, it won't help. She asked, "How is this being spread? Did I do something? Is the community blaming me?"

He looked at her with shock, "Oh, hell, no! This problem started twenty years ago when pigs from Mexico were brought up to Missouri. This farmer knew that pigs were dirt cheap down there. Easy money! They were all infected, but no one knew until after he had bred several hundred piglets and sold all over the Midwest. Don't know how they were able to track this strand down to that particular instance but that is what they are saying."

Judy thanked him, took the mail, and said good-bye. He told her to come to church Sunday, we miss her, and it would do her good to get out.

Judy sat the mail down. The conversation made her feel better, but still didn't fix the problem of no income. What does she do? She glanced through the mail, bills, advertisement, papers, and then an answer to a prayer letter from Ben.

She opened it. There was a black and white photo in the envelope of Ben sitting on a jeep. He looked so handsome. Judy could tell he was tired, lost weight, but there he was smiling at her. His letter was very good, almost happy. He has not seen a lot of battles. The Germans and Italians seem to be weakening. Their supplies have been cut off by the English, so it is working in their favor.

Then he kept asking about her. How are things going? I hope the cows aren't kicking you with your cold hands, ha-ha.

Judy didn't know what to do. How does she tell him? She didn't want to tell him through a letter. He needs to be focused on being safe, not on me here in Iowa. She started to write him back. It was a very short letter, and I had a conversation with Bud, the mailman. I am going to church with him and his wife. There will be a social afterwards. I felt good at the invite. I decided to start building up our social network for when you get home. After I have had you all to myself for a month, we will need to interact with society. I can't wait until you get home. I need you here safe and sound. Please take care and don't worry about me here. I am fine.

Judy wondered if he would be able to read between the lines how she kept saying she was fine. Not the farm, not the dogs, not the cows, etc.

As she was folding the letter and putting a stamp on the envelope, she saw the instructions from the previous letter concerning the blessing that the lady from Egypt had given him. She thought to herself, *What the hell? It couldn't hurt. I am going to church to pray for forgiveness tomorrow anyway.*

She went out to the trash barrel, covered her fingers in soot and came back into the kitchen. She drew the symbol on the four walls of the four directions. She drew a circle in the center of the room. The instructions had an incantation written out, but she didn't understand it. A copy of this letter was in the archives when researching the family. The language looked like a mix of Latin and French.

Judy washed her hands and went to bed. For the first time in months, she slept peacefully.

# CHAPTER 27

When Sunday rolled around, Judy got into the tub and soaked for a long time. This was the first time she had cleaned herself in over a week. She was getting sick of her own stench. There were no chores, so she was able to just sleep longer.

She stepped out of the tub, got dressed for church and the cloud of depression seemed to be somewhat lighter. She rode her bike to church, she wanted to save on gasoline since she is running out of money. Judy and Ben did not attend church other than Easter and Christmas, but the invitation that someone might want to see her felt too good to pass up. She also thought since she is in a bad way at home, prayer couldn't hurt.

As she walked in the service, everyone turned their heads to look at her. It wasn't her imagination. The looks weren't of a judgment/ *What the hell are you doing here?* – type of feeling; it was more of a *We are glad to see you, we care* feeling.

There is always coffee and donuts after Sunday service. Church is over at ten-thirty, so everyone goes to the basement and talks and gossips for a while before heading home to their Sunday meal.

Judy was approached by a woman who owned the local restaurant. Shirley was in her mid-forties and a very wise woman. She never married, lived alone, but was regarded as the wise lady in town both in business and personal life.

Shirley told Judy that she had heard about the situation with the animals and how it was affecting most of the counties in Iowa. Shirley asked what Judy had heard from Ben. They continued to share stories and Judy was actually enjoying her conversation with Shirley. She didn't realize how alone she had kept herself.

Shirley ended the conversation with a job offer. "Judy, I need someone who can wait tables. I need more but I know you are very young, but you need an income and I need help. Do you think you could come work for me? You will get an hourly wage of thirty-five cents, plus any tips you get."

Judy was surprised, a smile came on her face. "I didn't know what I was going to do since we have no livestock anymore. I have no skills. Thank you for being willing to do this. Yes, do you need me today?"

Shirley smiled, "No, I stay open very late on Saturday nights, so Sundays we are closed. Be at my place by 5:00 A.M. tomorrow morning. I will give you a quick lesson, and we'll be ready for the breakfast crowd."

The two women left the church and Judy rode her bike home. She felt like church was definitely the right thing to do. She was in the kitchen trying to be creative with what little groceries she had to prepare a meal and as she walked across the circle, her head felt squeezed, her heart tightened, and she thought she heard murmuring. A very low deep voice chanting. She regained her balance and stepped out of the circle. Her cheeks started to turn red, she felt embarrassed in her own home alone because as she was in the circle, she also felt orgasmic. The picture of many hands and tongues all over her, wanting her made her blush.

# Chapter 28

Judy had a knack for service. She caught on very quickly to the restaurant business. The customers fell in love with her wit, which she herself didn't know she had. Her tips added up to an amazing haul for her every day. She never wanted to take a day off. When autumn came around, she had to take a day off to run the combine on her sixty acres. That only took a couple days to combine, dry, and sell the corn.

This gave her enough money to put in savings. She felt like maybe a new car someday would be a good investment because it will start to snow soon and riding a bicycle would not be a good idea.

A year went by and Ben's letter said that he was coming home in thirty days. Judy was so excited; she had saved enough money for Ben to buy some livestock when he got back. She had told him about her job, and he was happy to know she is taking care of herself. Ben kept talking about Judy and him raising a family when he got home. Judy never would respond about that; she was loving the business world too much and really did not want kids.

Shirley was getting sick a lot lately. She was teaching Judy about bookkeeping, ordering food, and making sure no one takes advantage of her. Personnel management, taxes, and license renewals are all organized by date to help keep organized.

Judy thought that Shirley was just wanting extra help and that Judy showed she could be a good manager. But one night, Shirley told Judy that she had cancer and wouldn't be around long. Judy was going to inherit the restaurant. Shirley had a long time boyfriend who was in the restaurant all the time he wasn't at work. Judy just figured he would get the restaurant. Shirley said that Larry had no interest in it, and he would just sit in here and drink the profits.

A month later, Shirley passed away. There was a funeral, then the restaurant held a reception afterwards. Larry was there, drinking a lot and pouring a lot for many people. Judy was running around making sure bowls of food were kept full, everyone felt comfortable. This was the one way Judy felt she could honor Shirley. She always wanted people to feel comfortable in her business. There was lots of laughter, storytelling, it was a good reception.

A few hours later, everyone had left except for Judy and Larry. They cleaned up and Judy was surprised how much Larry helped. They were getting ready to leave and Larry held the door open for Judy. She turned around to lock up when Larry said, "Let me give you a ride home." Judy did not want to ride with him, but she was dead tired.

"Okay, I am tired, even though it isn't very far. Thanks," Judy said.

Larry took this opportunity while he had her in the pickup to say, "I know why Shirley left you the restaurant and not me. I would have no idea how to run it, you seemed to thrive ever since you started working for her. I know you will do the best for Shirley's memory. It couldn't be in better hands."

Judy was so relieved; she was a little nervous about seeing Larry ever since Shirley told her about the idea of giving Judy the place. "I am so pleased you feel that way, Larry. I was surprised when Shirley told me. I didn't want you to think I bullied my way into her business."

Larry said, "As long as I can still have my spot at the bar, you won't have any problems with me."

Judy chuckled and replied, "Nothing will change. You're welcome to the restaurant just exactly as if Shirley were still physically here with us."

This comment caused a change in Larry's face and Judy noticed it. She turned her head and stared out the windshield while she started hugging the passenger door. They turned into the driveway and Judy thanked him and got out as quickly as she could.

Larry stepped out of his pickup and asked if he could use her bathroom, he needed to head out to one of his farms and it was twenty miles away. He drank too much punch at the reception. She really did not want him in her house but how can you say no to someone who needs to pee.

"Sure," she said. They walked in the front door together and she pointed to the back of the house to where the bathroom was. She took off her coat and put it on the coat rack by the door. She walked into the kitchen and started to make some coffee. She needed to catch up on the books since Shirley died, it was difficult to keep up with everything. That was four days ago, but it was time to get back to reality. She was standing at the counter with her back to the living room door when she felt hands slide around her waist. She swung around and Larry was pulling her in to kiss her forcefully. Judy put her hands on his shoulders to push him back. "You said nothing would change, just as if Shirley were still here. So, here I am." He started to grab her breasts, tear at her clothes, she pushed him back and as he stepped back, she was pulled forward.

He eventually stepped into the circle on the floor. He had his hand on Judy's arm. The floor started to shake like something was trying to burst through the floorboards. Judy was able to yank free of his hold as he was frozen staring down at his feet. Judy ran into the living room, but she stayed just outside the door to the kitchen because there was absolutely no sound or vibrations outside of the kitchen.

Larry tried to keep his balance, spreading his arms and feet. He saw Judy standing outside the door and lunged for the door, but as he did, a large tentacle burst through the floor and grabbed his legs. He rolled onto his back and screamed. While Larry thrashed around and tried to free himself, other tentacle's burst through making the hole in the floor larger.

The tentacles were black and looked like they were covered in an oily muddy fluid. The hole in the floor looked muddy and deep. Larry's arms and legs were all held down and spread apart. Another creature was crawling out of the hole. It felt as if the devil himself was coming for a visit.

This creature had a large, bird-like body. It looked like a month old roadkill sprung to life except it was over six feet tall. It looked like the torso was ripped open and maggots crawling all over it. Judy's eyes drifted up to the head of the creature and it looked like a cat. Judy fell; she was terrified and couldn't move. The creature looked at her, didn't move toward her but she would swear it smiled at her.

The thing looked down at Larry, there was a scream coming out of the creature, but it sounds like a low demonic growl. At the same time, Larry was screaming and cursing. The cat-bird thing opened his mouth and with the largest fangs ever seen, pounced on Larry, ripping his flesh off of his body. Blood was spraying all over the house. Larry was still alive. The creature was tearing at the muscle and picking at it exactly like the birds do on the highway. Arteries and veins were being bitten and blood splattering in a beat rhythm.

Larry blood and screaming stopped. The cat thing looked at Judy, she thought it was bowing to her and jumped back down inside the hole. The tentacles wrapped around Larry and pulled him down. A person could hear the bones crushing as his body was folded in half. All quiet.

Judy sat there in shock. Eventually she got up, walked carefully to the hole, and peered down to see something. All she saw was darkness. Judy stepped back, replaying everything in her mind, and looked around the room. She noticed some things right away. The symbols had blood sprayed all around them but not a single drop was on the symbol. Then she looked down at the circle she drew. The hole and broken floorboards were only inside the circle, almost like the edge was a barrier.

The lines of the symbols and the circle was made from soot, but now it looked almost like it was starting to burn into the wood. Judy shook herself into reality and got on her knees and started moving dirt into the hole. She threw the floorboards into the hole. She ran out to the back yard where she knew there was some plywood and brought it to the house. She nailed it over the hole. Then she started scrubbing the kitchen. She was using bleach to get rid of the blood. There was no way she was going to call this in. No one would believe her; they would just figure Judy killed him for his advances.

She waited until the middle of the night when her neighbors would be asleep to go out and move his truck. She lifted her bicycle into the back and drove it out to his home place. It was around 1:00 A.M. at this time. She got on her bike and rode it back to town. Luckily, she knew he lived on a farm that was only seven miles out of Lenox. He had several but his home was on this one.

# CHAPTER 29

The next day, Judy got to work and tried to act like she knew nothing about Larry. A few weeks went by, but they couldn't find Larry. He was missing. No evidence was discovered, nothing showed up in the truck.

The strangest thing happened. One of her neighbors passed away but their will had Judy's name on it. She told the lawyers that it had to be a mistake because she didn't know them enough other than to say Hi. They said the will was changed around the time Shirley changed her will.

Judy now had over five hundred acres. She was able to rent the land and was making money. Ben came home, and when she explained the events of the symbols and Larry, the land, restaurant, he realized what the "blessing" had been. As long as they bring a sacrifice, a human, to the circle, they would be making money.

Sometimes a stranger would show up in the restaurant, and they would use that person as the sacrifice. They first struggled with this idea, but the money became a disease and greed changed their personalities. They agreed no children should be brought into the home.

They decided to stay in that small house, not to put on airs. They had millions of dollars in just a few years. They became suspicious of anyone wanting to get to know them. They were eventually known as horrible people.

One night Judy noticed a group of women her age eating together, having a girl's night out. This ripped Judy's heart out. Ben and she had each other but no other friends. They were lonely, but they knew they had to keep everyone away from them for their own safety.

Judy went home and asked Ben if they could just rip off the symbols, get rid of them. They had had over one hundred deaths (sacrifices) and she realized that money was not making them happy. Ben agreed, they ripped off the boards where the symbol and circle was, but it was underneath. Every time they tore up a board, there would be another board under it.

They decided to burn the house down. One night, they spread gasoline all over it and set it on fire. They drove away and went to Des Moines for the night.

The next day, they drove back to Lenox expecting to see a crowd around their house and nothing but smoldering wood in place of the house. They turned off Main Street heading toward their house and didn't see any activity. They pulled up in front of their house and couldn't believe their eyes. It looked exactly the same. They ran inside expecting to smell gasoline, but there was none.

They could not get rid of the "blessing." They ended up spending the rest of their lives with millions of dollars and zero friends. They became bitter and angry at the whole world. Ben died in 1967 and Judy died in 1969. Their will stated that their money would go to their nieces and nephew who lived in Florida. The one stipulation was that no one would ever live or step foot in the house and it would never be torn down.

# Chapter 30

I got it now, the house has become so broken down that Katie was able to pry the door open and she stepped into the circle. This means that they are still there to this day. I had to figure out a way to deactivate the power.

Since this was Egyptian, a regular Christian exorcist would probably not work. Further research led to an interesting discovery; the demon was called Kroni. It actually was Hindu. Kroni was born with multitudinous limbs each the size of a mountain and was the first evil to be born in the Universe. This demon was similar to Kali except it has a cat head with large fangs. Kroni feeds off of blood and producing chaos. The lore states that if Kroni is fed blood willingly, she will stop.

The was confusing since the people murdered were drained of their blood.

The key is the word "willingly." Could it be that simple? I need to try. I need tons of blood to pour in the circle without getting killed myself. How?

Finding dead bodies with their blood is impossible to do. The only dead bodies would be from nursing homes, but how would I gain access to them. I called Kelli and asked her to come to Lenox. She has been with me on all of our investigations. I needed someone to brainstorm solutions with.

While I was waiting for Kelli to arrive, I called a Hindu Temple in NYC. I explained that (lied) I was doing a thesis on comparisons between Christian, Buddhism, and Hindu religions. The goal is to put mutual respect on all forms of worship towards each other.

I think he must have bought it because we had a long conversation. In summary, Kali is considered a Goddess. Hindus still prayed to her to this day. My thought was defeating a God would be a whole new ball game than a ghost or demon.

I asked if he knew anything about Kroni. He was a demon that thrived on blood and destruction. But the strange thing, the lore stated that if he gets too much of a good thing, he leaves. His appetite grows only if the taking of the blood is horrific. If it were calm or peaceful, he would be unsatisfied and disappear. It is the strangest think he has ever read about a demon, but there was no other documentation saying anything different.

# CHAPTER 31

Kelli showed up and we went straight to work. It took several hours to bring her up to speed with my discoveries. Trying to figure out how to over-feed this demon with blood was definitely a problem.

We got hungry, so we decided to drive to Creston to a restaurant. There really in only a couple of places to eat in Lenox and I had enough of greasy burgers.

This was a twenty-minute drive on Hwy 34. Kelli and I were talking about solutions. We were so tired that hungry that our solutions were more of a comedy act. Getting blood out of turnips, ha-ha. All the men that broke up with us, lead them to the circle. The movie Carrie came to mind, pour pigs blood into the circle. We were going crazy with no idea in the near future.

I was rounding the curve just next to the Chicken House, an old restaurant and dance hall from many decades ago and there was a truck in front of me. I had to slow down since this trucker decided to go the speed limit and I never like to go that slow.

Our conversation stopped, we went ten miles without speaking then we looked at each other and said, "That is the answer. A tanker of pig's blood from a meat packing plant."

We got to the restaurant and I had my briefcase with me. As we waited on our food, we went over the notes to see if there was anything about what type of blood was needed? Why couldn't it be pig's blood? Pigs actually have more in common with the human body's physical make up than other farm animals. If this doesn't work, I will try to explain it to Kroni as he is devouring me.

Ok, this is an idea and possibly a working idea. Both Kelli and I work in a community with a very large packing plant. They take tankers out daily. I found out that the tanker hold over eleven thousand gallons of blood. That should equal overfeeding. How do we get a tanker? Do we hijack a truck? We have no idea how to drive an eighteen wheeler or to dump the liquid.

I called the parent of a student from our school who is in the security department for the plant. I can trust her; she is kind of a bad ass, so I know asking questions would not be a problem. I asked about the tankers, how would one be able to disappear, how could it be delivered to a different location?

She said that the logbooks for the trucks are very strict now a days due to everything being monitored electronically and GPS. I needed a driver that is not very reliable but still working. She knew exactly who to suggest.

I looked at Kelli and I told her that I would be breaking the law and if she wanted to just go home, I would understand. I explained that I was going to go back to the plant, wave him down as he drove out of the plant. I was going to ask him to help me with my car that was broken down on the highway. I knew this individual, he would love to help, thinks all women who talk to him are flirting and he has weak morals.

The next time he was scheduled to drive the tanker was in three nights. This was perfect. Kelli decided to help me. She dropped me off at the gate of the plant and she drove the car out to Hwy 30. I saw the truck pull out and I walked in front to make sure he would stop. I called him out by name, which this excited him: "Zack, I hear you are the hero I need right now. I was told you could stop and help me with my car that is broken down out by Iowa Protein. Isn't that where you are taking this blood?"

Zach was probably mid-fifties, very skinny. He has a substance problem but seems to be able to keep a job. He is single, is known to try to get some of the strippers from the club to go home with him. He is kicked out a few times a year from the club. I knew if I flirted very hard with him, he would not question me. He responded, "Sure, sweetheart, climb on in, and I'll help ya. I can fix anything." I gagged on "sweetheart," but I put on my happy face and climbed in.

I showed him where my rental car was, and he pulled over right behind the car. Kelli was laying in the back seat preparing the drink. She put some sleeping powder in some beer to put him to sleep. Not to hurt him but to gain control over the truck. He walked over to the front of the car, looked around, connected some cables that Kelli disconnected, and it fired right up.

I got really excited and hugged him. "Thank you so much. I have a six pack of Bud Lite; would you please have a drink with me in gratitude for helping me?

He said, "Sure, I could drink one." I explained that I have never drank beer in the bed of a truck and would he mind letting me climb in there?

I thought his eyes were going to pop out. Kelli gave me the beer and the one with no cap was the one to give him. I gave it to him and opened one myself. I pretended to drink as he downed the beer. At least he had the sleeping meds in him right away. I opened another one for him. I wanted to keep his hands busy.

We talked, twenty minutes later, he was slurring, and I invited him to lay in the bed. He was out. Kelli had experience driving an eighteen-wheeler from working on the farm, so she got behind the wheel, I got in the rental car and we drove off. I parked the car in the Walmart parking lot, no one cares what goes on there. I got in the truck and we drove to Lenox, a long, two-hour drive.

# CHAPTER 32

As we drove into town, it was around midnight. I knew that no law enforcement was in town. The county sheriff was in Bedford at this time. Thank you, cousin, for telling me the scheduling of patrolling. I told Kelli that we would be more hidden if she drove in the alley behind the house. There were no streetlights and the kitchen where the circle was is in the back of the house.

Kelli did a great job, there were a few grinding gears, but we made it. I got out and grabbed the hose and connected it to the drainage spout at that back of the truck. We had no idea how to work this, but it didn't seem too complicated. I locked the hose onto the spout, took the other end of the hose into the kitchen. The circle was just two feet beyond the length of the hose. "Fuck!"

Kelli came in and looked at the problem. She immediately went outside. I thought she was going to run away. She came back in with part of a rain gutter from the side of the house. "Oh, my God, thank you!" It was not a perfect fit, but it should work fine.

We decided that Kelli would turn on the pump on the truck and I would hold the hose and gutter to the circle. How long did it take to empty eleven thousand gallons of blood? We were about to find out. If the hole was as deep as they mentioned, it should empty fairly fast.

I connected the gutter; it was held over the hole in the circle and Kelli was told to start 'er up. I could feel the blood rushing, the hose was bouncing way too much. A stream of blood came rushing out and I lost hold of it and the gutter slipped off. Blood was spraying everywhere, all over the kitchen, the windows, and I was drowning in blood. The hose was six inches in diameter, so the force of the spray was overwhelming. I was able to hug the hose, Kelli came running in and grabbed the gutter and between the two of us, the blood was spraying into the hole. Kelli was covered also. I started laughing, thinking of Carrie again, "Hey, just think...we are both prom queens!"

I was receiving one of Kelli's famous dirty looks. I looked at her and asked, "Do you feel that? Is the floor vibrating?" She said it was probably just from the truck and the pump. I didn't think so. I looked down at where she was sitting, and she was in the circle.

I freaked out. "Get out of the circle!" Just at the same time, the slimy and bloody arms came out of the hole. The stench and horror of what we were seeing paralyzed us. I reached over and pushed Kelli really hard away from the demon. I yelled at her to get out of the house. She refused, I told her that I was not in the circle, so I was going to be okay. I lied, lied really bad but it got her to leave.

I didn't know if the demon was extra hungry or what but the lore of being in the circle didn't seem to matter. It crawled out of the hole; a limb reached to grab me. The blood was not going in the hole anymore since I could not hold the gutter to the hose by myself. I did not want Kelli to get killed.

I decided the gutter was not helping the situation. I backed up and grabbed the hose with both arms and was able to direct the spray to the mouth of the demon. It had been twenty minutes already and the tanker was only one-third empty. The screams from the demon were deafening. It was so loud that I couldn't even hear the truck or the blood being pumped out of the hose. `I was starting to panic, then the research came into my mind. Kroni loves chaos. The more chaos the hungrier it became. The thought of talking to it like a puppy came into my crazy mind to try to be calm. I didn't think I could do it, but it was try or be killed.

I sat down on the floor outside the circle, still holding the hose as it pumped more gallons of blood. I tried to take a deep breath, but my nose and mouth were full of blood. I started talking out loud by saying things like, "I heard you were hungry. I got this food for you. I hope this makes you happy. Just lay back and enjoy the taste of this wonderful blood."

No more fake nice thoughts came to me, so I started singing. I couldn't think of anything except, "Jesus loves me, yes, I know." Several minutes later, the monster stopped screaming. I could tell the tanker was getting close to empty based on the calming of the hose and the fact that it was getting easier to hold.

Kroni stopped waving the limbs around, stopped screaming. It started to be still, slowly started to descend into the hole. Kelli came in to see why it was getting quieter, she saw that the demon was disappearing into the hole. The blood was started to become less and less. I didn't want to take any chances, so I told Kelli to grab the hose while I grabbed the gutter to make sure the rest gets into the hole. I wanted to drown it.

It was twenty minutes later when we shut off the pump. We just stood there staring into the hole, trying to see or hear anything. We did not speak, we walked out to the truck, wound up the hose, secured it. Climbed back into the truck, checked on sleeping beauty who was snoring. We drove back to our town. It would be around 5:00 A.M. when we arrived at the parking lot. Zach had lot of rolls of paper towels in the truck. We used them to sit on, we wiped down the traces of blood we left. We took them with us. We parked the truck, so that any video of us getting out and into my rental would be blocked by the truck.

The plan was always to leave Zach and the truck in the parking lot. It would look like his truck was hijacked. He might be fired but he told me during our short romance that he was changing jobs anyway.

I drove Kelli to her Jeep and we parted ways. I thanked her, told her that I was going to keep our records. I have a funny feeling that we may need this information again. We parted ways, went home, showered for a really long time.

Kelli doesn't know this but before we left Lenox, I started a fire in the living room. If it burned down, then that was a sign that we were successful. I hope Katie can rest and go into the light now. I am so sorry.

# Epilogue

The summer has been busy with traveling for fun and ghost hunting. We stayed locally within the state. We bought some fancy new equipment. Because of our short-lived fame the businesses were willing to give us a big discount as long as we mentioned them on our blog/ YouTube. Kelli and I have been able to talk a lot about what happened. Zach was not fired, he told them about some woman who drugged him. The fact that blood was not found was an issue that just kind of freaked the bosses out. Zach was given a different duty, but he quit anyway. I felt bad about what I did but I don't feel bad about the result.

I have not found out anything about the house since we left town. The legendary Rodeo was the last weekend in July. I thought I would go down to visit old friends but to see about the house. I was nervous, what if it did not work.

I drove into town, turned down main street. I was stalling, there was a faster way to get to the site, but I was dreading to see the aftermath. I turned down the road towards the house, three blocks away. Everything seemed normal so far. My stomach was churning, if it didn't work, I was out of ideas.

One block to go, the space between my grandparents' old house and the one two lots away seemed farther apart. I stopped, pulled over to the side. The house was gone, the burnt remains were gone but the charred earth was still there. I got out, walked over to the site, and looked for the deep hole.

Nothing.

It was as though it never existed. Thank God. I got back into my car, started to think about the amount of death this creature caused. The amount of death the greedy son - of -bitches from years past that let this happen.

Then I started to think of Katie. Lost Trail caused a death. A game that was so much fun, created such wonderful memories. Katie who was just looking for acceptance. Her life was sad. The feelings took me over. I started to cry, then erupted with such sadness that I could not stop.

I drove home, I couldn't go to the Rodeo. I got home, said a Rosary on behalf of Katie. I slept. The next day, the phone rang. The manager of the library in Michigan that we investigated before was calling. Strong activity has begun at the library again, but much more vicious. Could we come up and investigate?

This time I am ready and armed with knowledge.